993258

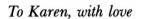

To Karen, with love

And he opened the bottomless pit; and there arose a smoke out of the pit, as the smoke of a great furnace; and the sun and the air were darkened by reason of the smoke of the pit.—Revelation 9:2

NOW

CHAPTER ONE

"Manley James found it all on Monday afternoon.

"He saw the buzzards floating overhead like his grandchildren's kites every time he looked up from painting the barn that morning, dark shadows on the bright blue October canvas.

"He saw them out the kitchen window while he ate the luncheon-meat sandwiches his wife fixed for him. And he smelled the smoke, even inside. Thicker than usual. Finally, at 1 o'clock, drowsy and wanting a nap, he decided he'd better see what Avery Booth was up to.

"As he got nearer, the smoke became heavier, and he had to take out the handkerchief and put it over his mouth and nose while he steered the pickup with one hand. The cinders burned worse than they ever had before. Rounding the last turn into Red Top, Manley saw that the buzzards' attention were attracted by something off to his left, something he could get a whiff of even from the road, even through all the smoke.

"Up ahead, he could barely make out the house through the haze, and he thought at first it was on fire. But then he saw that the smoke was coming from out back, on beyond the barn, and he realized that it was the sawdust.

"The only sounds Manley James heard were Avery's old mongrel barking, hoarse and steady as a clock, and a kind of sizzling sound behind that. He got out of the truck and fought the smoke until he reached the barn where so many people had stood and sat that summer, and then he saw that the big orange mountain wasn't there any more.

"It seemed to have imploded, like one of the buildings Manley would see once in a while on TV. He walked up to the edge of it, and he could see that it was burning in serious

9

now, exposed to the air after smoldering underneath all that time.

"He was about to turn around and go looking for Avery Booth when he saw something shine in the midst of all the gloom. He couldn't make it out until he got 10 feet away, and then he saw that it was a ring, and that the ring was attached to a finger and thus a hand sticking out of the smoldering sawdust.

"Manley ran, wheezing, to his truck, but before he could get in and start back to call the fire department or the rescue squad or the sheriff, he noticed the buzzards again. He walked out across Avery Booth's yard, over toward where they were circling and squatting and eating. And this time he didn't have to get 10 feet away, or even 100, before he saw what it was, before he saw that it wasn't a dog or a possum or even a cow that the birds were feasting on.

"'Great gawd awmighty,' the old man said. He'd broken into a sweat that a breeze now turned into goosebumps. And when one of the birds, startled by a human presence, gave out with a sharp sound, it was so like a laugh that Manley never looked back until Red Top was out of sight."

Nancy looks up, relieved. All done. There is polite clapping.

"Anyhow, that's how it starts."

"Thank you, Ms. O'Neil," the president of the women's club says, giving Nancy a smile and a slight jerk of her head that tells her it isn't time to sit down, much as Nancy wants to. She hasn't sung enough for her supper yet. "Now, are there any questions?"

Front row, third from the left: "How long did it take you to write 'Egypt'?"

Hard question, Nancy thinks. "It depends. Either five months" (she realizes she's saying EYE-ther instead of EE-ther and hopes Suzanne and Marilou don't start snickering) "or 20 years, according to how you look at it."

Nancy can tell that this is taken for Writer Being Cryptic, but before she can explain, another hand shoots up, third row from the back, in the middle:

"Where did you find the time?" There's a murmur around the room, as if that was everybody's next question. If they only knew how long it had all been building up, how I'd work it all out in my head, just like it happened, Nancy thinks. A frontal lobotomy wouldn't have made it go away.

She resists the urge to tell the woman, "The time found me," and gives her stock answer about time management and an understanding family.

Everything changed so fast and so much afterward, and so much of it was tied to writing, that she never wanted to put a piece of paper in a typewriter again.

And, if Holly hadn't died in February and if Sebara hadn't reappeared in April, almost 20 years to the day after it all started, it might still be locked up inside my head, Nancy thinks to herself. So, like Dr. Jamison suggested, she just turned on the computer and let it flow, stranger than fiction.

Second row, all the way to the right: "Does being a librarian help you as a writer? I mean, all those books and all . . ."

Yeah, Nancy thinks to herself, if I'd really wanted to get away from writing, why did I get a master's in library science, the cheapest master's in the Western Hemisphere? Just look at my paycheck if you don't believe it. Like the doc said, there must have been some subconscious part of me that still wanted to write, in spite of everything that happened.

She staggers through 20 minutes of it, her first reading and Q-and-A, her words echoing off the 20-foot ceilings as the air conditioning goes on and off every five minutes. Finally, mercifully, the club president says, "One more question."

A woman about 50, about my age, Nancy thinks, raises her hand:

"I've heard that some of what you wrote about in 'Egypt' was from first-hand experience. Could you talk about that?"

Had to happen. Richmond's not that big . . .

"No," Nancy tells her, trying to be polite. God knows, she thinks, I don't want to hurt the feelings of any potential $19.95-a-book customers. "I don't think I could talk about that. All I can say is that I've known some interesting people, and a piece of some of them is in the book."

And a big chunk, she thinks to herself, of one in particular, one black-eyed, red-haired demon that wouldn't stay buried.

Lot Chastain, she wishes, rest in peace. Please?

11

1971

CHAPTER TWO

The window was up, because it was one of those rare April days when springtime in Virginia is more than a myth, so Nancy heard the Duster that Sam had bought the month before as it pulled into the gravel driveway, scattering a spray of stones into the grass, and she heard him slam the door, hard. It wasn't yet two, so she thought maybe the night pharmacist was sick and Sam was taking a quick hour off before he had to pull double duty again.

She could hear him fumbling with the keys. Sam said that having to have a deadbolt made him feel as if he were living in New York City instead of Richmond, but it was he who had insisted on it when they moved to the North Side four years before. Nancy was a city girl; a bump in the basement or a car door slammed three houses away didn't bother her, then.

The floor squeaked as he walked across the carpet and up the stairs, same as always.

Wade, who had learned to say "Daddy" before even "Mommy," called out to Sam as he passed by the upstairs bath, sputtering the word with water dripping down his face. But Sam walked right past, still wearing his white pharmacist's coat with the name bar. He usually took it off before he got to the parking lot as he left work. He didn't speak to either his wife or his two-year-old son, just walked straight into the bedroom.

Nancy heard closet doors and drawers being yanked open. She gave Wade's hair a rough drying-off, left him sitting in the tub, and walked down the hall, expecting the worst.

Sam was standing in front of his sock drawer, picking out all the pairs he could find and throwing them into the biggest suitcase they owned.

15

20115715

Nancy watched him pack a dozen pairs of socks and five or six singles, in case they matched. Then he started on the underwear.

"Sam?" Nancy said. "Honey?"

He didn't answer the first time, so she tried again. Finally: "What?"

"Are you running away from home?"

He almost smiled.

"We all are," he said. "We're moving."

Nancy looked at her husband for a sign. He used to play practical jokes. But all she saw now was a mind already made up.

She was quiet for a moment, then asked, "Where?" for lack of anything better.

"Monacan. You better get moving. Bus leaves in half an hour."

What finally did it was tampons.

Sam Chastain was, until April of 1971, head pharmacist for one of DrugLand's two West End stores. After two drinks, he would tell anybody who would listen that he wasn't really a pharmacist, just an office manager, the guy who hired and fired the checkout girls and counted the inventory. Most of the clerks missed a couple of days a month with cases of the flu that usually struck on Fridays or Mondays, according to which way the weekend needed to be stretched.

Sam really hated Mondays. On Mondays, any underpaid DrugLand worker was liable to call in sick.

He felt things should resolve themselves without human intervention whenever possible, at home or at work, so he never fired anyone, no matter how many times they shagged and spilled beer on the Work Ethic. When Sam Chastain came home and started packing, Nancy knew things had gone far beyond irritating.

The Monday it happened, he told Nancy that Etta Culbreth had called at five minutes 'til 9. It was supposed to reach 80 degrees by mid-afternoon, which it did, not a cloud in the sky. She called to tell Sam she was stuck in Virginia Beach with car trouble. Her transmission, she thought. It meant that Sam would have to stock the store, between prescriptions, while the girl who wasn't planning on being sick until Friday ran the cash register.

He was in the small section of the store that actually sold products related to the human body. He was tearing into a box of super tampons when he looked up and saw he was waist-high to Miss Mosby High of 1956, who was in town shopping. Corinne Cobb was wearing a pink miniskirt that hinted she had a better body than she did in high school, where Sam worshipped her pointed, bra-contoured breasts and golden-haired presence from afar.

Nancy was pretty sure that Sam was not cool in high school, not like Buddy and she had thought they were. In the yearbooks she looked at, Sam was on the track team and the debate team, but he wasn't in any of those spontaneously posed pictures that every yearbook staff always has taken of the "right" crowd. He was voted Most Studious.

But Sam always felt he was a late bloomer, somebody who would someday make all those cheerleaders and majorettes moan, "I didn't know THAT was Sam Chastain."

Now, though, on his knees wrestling with a box of super tampons, a little bit of a beer gut hanging over the belt of his white shirt, he saw the look on Corinne Cobb's face just before she turned and walked away without a word, and he knew that his life might not be yielding all he'd hoped it would. He feared that maybe he was the same boy he was in high school, 14 years ago, and it really pissed him off. He blamed DrugLand for placing him, a Trained Pharmacist, in such a compromising position.

Sam left the keys with the clerk and called Tim Litwin, his supervisor. He told him he had the flu.

Then he picked up his coffee mug and his briefcase, and he left.

From Richmond to Monacan was only 35 miles, but the suburbs fell away to country just past the last shopping center. By the time Sam, Nancy and Wade had gotten 10 miles from their brick colonial on the North Side, the woods were already starting to take over.

Wade sat in the back, just happy to be going to Grandma and Grandy's. Nancy looked out the window at a succession

FRANKLIN COUNTY LIBRARY
906 NORTH MAIN STREET
LOUISBURG, NC 27549
BRANCHES IN BUNN.
FRANKLINTON. & YOUNGSVILLE

of cinder-block houses, dammed-up ponds and service stations and wondered what the hell they were doing. The woods were the light, new green of spring, with white dogwoods everywhere. Nancy was 28 years old, four years younger than Sam. At this point in her life, it was still her normal inclination, when someone told her to do something, to turn around and do the opposite. But something about Sam's unblinking eyes, something about the absolute calm with which he prepared to move them all out of Richmond, convinced her that, for the time being, his mind was made up. He was going to Monacan, and he just assumed that she'd wrap up Wade and go with him.

Nancy knew enough about Sam's family to understand the Putting-Your-Foot-Down tradition. The men didn't say much, didn't make many decisions and yielded frequently on day-to-day things. The few times they did clench their jaws, though, she saw that they were treated as if they were privy to divine wisdom. Later, Nancy wrote it off as either an unwillingness to trample on hallowed Chastain tradition or the nagging feeling that she should have been more of a trouper in her first marriage. So she went along.

Besides, she told herself, Sam is always threatening to move back to Monacan.

Sam turned off the new interstate and approached town from the north. He drove his family across the river and past the drive-in theater, and then the water tower came into view, its faded red letters promising: "Monacan: Your Future's Here." Some high school kids had climbed it and painted "NOT" between and just above "Future's" and "Here." Nancy wasn't sure which prediction was least ominous.

Sam had been silent since they left Richmond. Finally, as they made the 45 degree turn that led off Route 17 and on to the road that would soon, around the bend, be Monacan's main street, he spoke.

"I can take over for Daddy," he told Nancy. "This is where we need to raise our family, right here where the kids can be with their Grandma and Grandy every day," and he looked back at Wade for confirmation. Wade was asleep.

Nancy wanted to say, "What about my family?" but something told her that this was a day to let it ride. It would take her years to stop depending on little voices of unknown origin for her guidance.

When they first met, Sam seemed to Nancy as if he were content to spend the rest of his life in Richmond. He was in the last year of pharmacy school then. He was 26 years old, with straight, dark hair and a sharp, chiseled French look that Nancy would come to notice in all the Chastain men she would know. His weak eyes and habit of squinting were all that kept him from handsome. Nancy was taking 12 hours at Richmond Professional Institute, trying to finish a degree in English for no apparent reason other than to show that she could finish something.

Sam was a blind date, on Valentine's Day. He and Nancy rolled around in the mud at fraternity parties, went to Virginia Beach just to eat fried shrimp and made love on top of a rather small mountain. Nancy loved Sam's dry wit; he made her laugh more than anything had in a long, long time. She thought he was a gift.

He got on well enough with Nancy's parents, although Suzanne did ask her one time, "What do you use to get him to talk, honey? Bamboo splints?"

It was true that Sam had never been much of a talker, unless he'd had too many gin-and-tonics. He and Nancy's father, Pat, could sit and watch nine innings of baseball on TV without the conversation going much beyond "Beer?" and "Yeah, thanks." He had a way, too, of getting up and walking out of the room at any time he was not being directly spoken to. This put off the O'Neils, or the female O'Neils at least, but Nancy explained to Suzanne and to her sisters, Marilou and Candy, that everybody in Sam's family was like that, even with each other. Nothing personal.

"It's just the Chastain in him," Pat would say, partly, Nancy felt, to drive her crazy. Pat was a great believer in blood, and he'd had a couple of Chastain brothers work for him at the cabinet shop.

"I saw Frank Chastain cut an inch off his little finger one day with a circular saw," he said, "and he didn't even yell. Just asked somebody to take him to the doctor. He was a smart worker, though."

Sam's saving grace, even the first couple of years they were married, was his penchant for the outrageous, made all the more outrageous because it came from the most deadpan man in Richmond.

The day of her 25th birthday, Nancy had a 10 a.m. class. Sam kissed her goodbye and gave her a card on his way out at 7:30. They were to go out to dinner that night.

On her way to the RPI campus, though, Nancy saw the first of the signs. She realized, by the time she got to the first main intersection, that there were three 25-mile-per-hour speed limit signs in their neighborhood, and that Sam had somehow managed to plaster a piece of white cardboard over the top of each, with black letters that matched those of the highway department, so that the signs read:

NANCY
CHASTAIN
IS
25

He never once conceded that it had been his doing, even after Nancy found the paint can in the basement.

"Must of been the birthday fairy," he maintained.

Her last two birthdays, Sam had been predictable as clockwork. He seemed to be too old—or too tired—for pranks any more. Nancy wrote it off to parenthood.

"He's not deadpan, sweetie," Suzanne told her over Thanksgiving. "He's just dead."

None of her children, after puberty, ever called Suzanne "Momma," and none of them, whatever age, called Pat anything except "Daddy." But it never seemed to bother Suzanne. She was 24 when Nancy was born, but by the time her oldest child was in her 20s, people were mistaking her and Nancy for sisters.

They had the same ash-blonde hair, the same slightly wide faces that turned beautiful into something between pretty and cute, the same toothy smile, the same impish blue eyes. But there was more to it than that. Suzanne never got tired, never failed to laugh at a dirty joke, never thought the music was too loud. "If it's too loud," she told Pat one time when he was complaining bitterly about the decibel level of one of Nancy's Buddy Holly records, "you're too old."

When they left Richmond that April day, Nancy didn't know whether Sam was going to turn around and go back, or if they were gone to the country for good. She packed three dresses, four blouses, four skirts, and some underwear and sweaters. She threw two coats in the back and hoped she wouldn't have to go back for her fall wardrobe.

But she did pack her homing novel, just in case.

Nancy had always liked to write. She won a sixth-grade fiction contest for all of Richmond. If Buddy Molloy hadn't asked her to marry him the day after they were graduated from high school, and if Nancy hadn't accepted and gone with him to Elizabeth City, North Carolina, to make it official, she probably would've gone to Richmond Professional Institute then, as several of her college-bound friends had.

But Nancy was what Suzanne called contrary, which always made her daughter cringe because it sounded so country. After Buddy and Nancy told Suzanne and Pat that they were married, Pat ran Buddy off and told Nancy that he wasn't paying her way to college unless they got "the thing" annulled. So, of course, Nancy stayed married. She and Buddy hung on for three years, she working as a waitress in Shockoe Slip, Buddy as a pressman at the Times-Dispatch. Nancy would catch a bus or a ride with a friend every day from their one-bedroom apartment west of the Boulevard, and she'd take a course or two at a time from RPI, determined to graduate out of spite.

She and her family stayed unreconciled for six months, but after Pat and Suzanne came over and got them on a sleet-slick Christmas day and forced them to have dinner with the O'Neil family, even had gifts for Buddy, the worst of that was over. Robbie, the youngest, had made her a book-stand in Pat's shop, and inside the card he attached, he wrote, "Please don't leave again." Pat even paid for some of Nancy's tuition. Later, Nancy wondered if she and Buddy would have done better if they'd had the common bond of railing against her hard-hearted family.

When Buddy and Nancy separated, she had 24 hours credit to show for three years of contrariness. She had $186 in a checking account and owed the school more than $1,000, even with Pat finally helping some. The only way her life had improved was that she was working in a higher class of restaurant.

But she had started to write. She would walk over to a restaurant three blocks away every weekday morning when Buddy had worked the night before and was sleeping late. It had red-and-white checkered window sashes and dark paneling, and some of the most interesting people in Richmond walked by on the sidewalk outside. If she was early enough, there'd be a seat by the window where she could drink hot tea. She would take out her lined notebook and write what she imagined was happening with all those people going by on the other side of the glass. After a couple of years, they'd reserve her a space—by the window on chilly days, near the shade in the back during the heat of summer.

The courses she took weren't a total waste, but there came a point where, in writing and in marriage, she realized that she was on her own. There was a brief affair that Buddy never learned about, with another student, but Nancy finally came to see infidelity as just more material, another character for another story.

She wrote short stories all the time, some of them good, some terrible. She'd turn a VCU professor with a Jewish last name into a survivor of the death camps who imported hams for a living; She'd remake the fat lady who cooked breakfast for early-bird workers into a former beauty queen living in the past; she even wrote a story from the viewpoint of the dachshund that hung around the back door whining for handouts.

At some undetermined time, it occurred to Nancy that she could put some of these characters together and maybe, just maybe, what she would have would be a novel. What came to her, offspring of a pair of short stories, was about a disintegrating family's trip to the New York World's Fair. She called it "Fair Chance." It soon was occupying much of her waking time.

Buddy and she had shared bodily fluids since the 11th grade, but he really didn't care much what she was writing or whether she was writing. She never pushed it on him, because he was always worn out after work and she was afraid he might laugh at her. Buddy never had any intentions of going to college. His father was a pressman, and he always assumed he'd be one, too. After a while, his friends and Nancy's friends didn't seem to have much in common unless they were among the precious few they still saw from high school. After a while, Buddy and Nancy didn't have much in common, either.

They argued a lot, both of them too young to ever give in. He was a good-looking boy, mischievous Irish face all dark and mysterious after he'd showered and shaved at noon, sometimes pulling Nancy back into bed with him if she wasn't at work or at school. But Buddy was a rover, even when he and Nancy were going steady in high school. She answered too many phone calls where there'd be silence on the other end, then a receiver softly replaced.

By the spring of 1964, not three years after graduation, Buddy moved out, and Nancy never tried very hard to get him back. He joined the Army after they filed for divorce, just in time for Viet Nam, and she gave up the apartment to live with a girlfriend near the campus. Nancy typed the rest of "Fair Chance" in four months in the back bedroom of her shared place in the Fan District. Buddy wrote her once from Fort Polk, Louisiana. She didn't write him back.

She worked up the nerve to ask one of her younger, less-intimidating professors to take a look at her novel. He kept it for three months, then told her that it was "very interesting," but that it started slowly and seemed not to go anywhere in particular. To Nancy, that seemed to pretty much cover things, but he said he thought it could be helped if it were written from the daughter's point of view.

So Nancy rewrote "Fair Chance," trying to "punch it up a bit" without really knowing how to, retelling the story through the eyes of a young girl not unlike her youngest sister, Candy.

23

This time, she got a list of regional publishers and started writing them, one at a time. The first one sent it back three months later with a letter that started "Dear Writer." "See," said Marilou, "they know you're a writer." The second one lost it. The third one actually sent a two-paragraph explanation of why "Fair Chance" was being rejected, which Nancy might have mistaken for progress if the letter hadn't noted that the story might best be told from the viewpoint of an omniscient observer.

"You know," said Marilou, two years younger and the second oldest, one Sunday when Nancy was having dinner with her family, "this novel of yours reminds me of that old homing pigeon Candy used to have. No matter how far away you sent the fucker, it'd always find its way home."

Suzanne tried to chastise Marilou, but everybody broke up, even Nancy. From then on, "Fair Chance" was known only as the homing novel.

Being the oldest, Nancy always felt guilty for setting what Pat had warned her once was a Bad Example for the rest. For years after Buddy and she got married and then slogged toward divorce court, she would try to impress Marilou and Candy and Robbie with how stupid they'd be to follow her sorry example. Whenever Robbie would get caught skipping school or Candy would get a "C," she could almost feel Suzanne and Pat blaming her. It was a great relief to Nancy when the other three "buckled down," more or less, even went to college and graduated, after which they hounded her to finish school.

That's OK, she thought. Better nagging than nagging guilt.

That day, turning off Route 17 onto the semicircular road that connected Monacan to the rest of the world, Nancy could only wonder what came next. She could find some solace in the fact that her husband had done something spontaneous for the first time in recent memory. She hoped that this was a good thing.

"We're going on an adventure, Wade," she whispered to their son as she picked him up out of the back seat in Sam's parents' driveway. "Daddy's taking us on an adventure."

24

CHAPTER THREE

*D*reamed that dream again last night, where I was eating fat lightning. It tasted salty as Smithfield ham, but bitter as gall, like when I used to bite down on the pencil in grade school and give it a little chew, and then Miss Watkins would make fun of me in front of class, the old bitch.

I wake up with a sourness in my mouth, thirsty like I've really been gnawing on wood instead of just dreaming about it, and my jaw hurts from chewing in my sleep. Funny thing is, it makes me want to get right up and eat something salty, bad as that fat lightning tastes in my sleep. I been eating salt herring and fatback for breakfast. And, you know, when I pick up a piece of fat lightning when I'm fixing to use it to start a fire, I look at the way you can see light through it, and damned if I don't feel like taking a bite.

I don't tell the girls or nobody about it, though. Ain't none of their business, and it'd be just like that hateful Aileen to have the rest of them gang up on me and try and get me put in Central State. I think they're already messing with my food. That corn Grace brought yesterday tasted right peculiar. They want to take Momma's house away from me, tear apart the sawdust pile, wipe everything clean like it never was here.

Oh, they got all kinds of tricks. Last week, they sent a man and a woman out here, said they was from the historical society, tried to fool me into thinking they was interested in fixing the old house up so folks could come and look at it and, she said, "See how the original settlers lived," like Daddy and Momma and their folks on back was something like you'd see in a zoo.

I know what they want. They want to sell this valuable land here, right on the river, make 'em all a bunch of money. Carter tries to tell me it ain't so, but I seen them fancy homes on the river in Richmond. I seen the big old mansion, big enough for a king, that that millionaire built between here and there. I ain't no fool.

When the man and woman are standing there, 'cause I won't let 'em in the trailer, he's kind of got his hand around her waist, and she ain't doing a blessed thing to stop him. They're probably whoring around together on the sly. Everybody does now. And God is going to put a stop to it right soon, you can be sure of that. Just like Sodom and Gomorrah. It just makes me sick. He ought to come and rain fire and brimstone on all of us, set our fields on fire. And he will, too.

But I told 'em right off they wouldn't be getting their hot little hands on the Chastain property any time soon. Momma left the house and the land right around it to me, not any of the rest. They all got their land, and done sold most of it, too. The history gal said it'd be my property until I died, or "passed on," as she put it. Said they'd just fix up the house some, improve the road in, so folks could see how the county used to be. Who they trying to fool? Soon as I sign a paper, they'll forge my signature on some deed and I'll have to move my trailer so Aileen and Carter and Grace and even little Holly—she's in on it, too—can make a fortune off this here land.

But I told the two of them, the history people, to haul their tails off my land before I sicced Granger on 'em. And Granger was already growling, hoping I'd let him off that chain I keep him on so he won't kill no more of Jeter's damn chickens, so they went on back to their Jap car and headed back out towards the highway.

And what's the matter with letting that sawdust pile go on and burn, is what I asked Carter the last time he come out here, saying the county wanted to haul it off or put it out, one or the other.

It's been burning for six years come July, and it ain't hurt a soul yet. Carter says folks are afraid it might cave in, that the volunteer fire department thinks it's a health hazard. So who's it going to cave in on? I asked Carter. It's half a mile out to where the road's even paved, and a mile more to Route 17. Long as the history folks don't turn me into a museum, who's going to be messing with my sawdust pile? They gonna ford the river at French Cross and trespass? If they do that, some of that white trash I seen playing and sitting across the river over by the train tracks, then it serves them right. Let 'em all fall in.

Besides, that sawdust pile burning reminds me of how it was when I was a boy and Daddy and them was running a working sawmill, way before we went broke in Hoover's time. The cinders and the

smoke gets in folks' eyes some, I reckon, but that'll teach 'em to stay
away from here, trying to take my land.

Even Carter, he asked me wouldn't it be nice to be able to move
back in the big house again, after they fixed it up? They'd let me do
that, he said.

It most surely would not be nice, I told him. When Momma died,
I moved out of that house. It was her house, and I don't aim to live
in it without her. I can't believe the things some people do, even your
own family, thinking it'll make you happy.

*Today, one of the cats has come skulking around here like she's
hiding something. Sure enough, I go back to the old barn, where I
know she likes to slip in between the cracks to get away from Granger
when I let him loose, and there's the kittens. Can't be more than two-
three days old, near-bout like little rats, five of them, all mewing
and all.*

*I run the momma cat off, which is not easy. "Ain't my fault," I
tell her. "I didn't go to it with some old Tom cat and bring all this
into the world." The momma hisses at me, but she knows better than
to mess with Lot Chastain. Yes, sir. I think about all them babies I
see on TV in that Biafra that ain't got enough to eat, and I get mad
at cats, the way they seem like they want to take over the world.*

*The burlap sack is laying on the ground over by the steps up to
the loft, where I left it last time. I get it and throw all the kittens
inside, all crying for their momma. I take it over to the wall, rear
back and slam it into the brick chimney. After about six times, I don't
hear no more crying, but I hit it six more just in case. The momma
cat has skulked around the corner, but I bet she's back when I put
the scraps out after supper.*

CHAPTER FOUR

The Chastains were all sitting on the front porch at Sam's parents' house, the first Sunday after the move. The porch was a good place to sit and rock until about 3 in the afternoon, when the sun dropped low enough to chase everybody to the back porch or inside for the rest of the day.

The houses in Monacan had been staggered so that, when you looked across the street, you looked not dead on at another house but at the space between two houses. Thus, you could see Main Street and the parking lot of the Chieftan Diner, a block away. Carter, Sam's father, liked to sit on the porch and try to figure out what was going on in town from the little swatch of it he could see. He said he learned more from the Chieftan Diner parking lot than he did from the Monacan Herald, which came out once a week.

"Looka there," he said, about 1:30. "There goes Boy Ed Stringfellow." Nancy could just make out a man getting into a Ford Torino, carrying what looked like Styrofoam containers. She could see him slam the door a split second before the sound swam to her in the already summer-humid air.

"Miss Mable must of found a hair in the hamburgers from Hardee's," he said. Nancy asked him how he knew that.

Carter smiled, glad that all his knowledge hadn't gone to waste. "She always makes Boy Ed go to Hardee's for Sunday dinner, and if it don't muster up, she sends him back to the diner."

Nancy offered that neither Hardee's nor the Chieftan Diner seemed like a great thing to depend on for Sunday dinner.

Carter explained that Miss Mable Stringfellow never cooked, that she had Boy Ed, her husband, bring everything from either Hardee's or the diner, because she didn't feel as if her stove was ever clean enough to cook on, no matter how much she scrubbed it. And then, half the time, she'd find something wrong with the take-out food.

Marie, Sam's mother, shook her head.

"Miss Mable's not right," she said.

Carter had spent most of his life observing Monacan and its residents. He seldom talked much, and never when you expected him to. He was the one who told Nancy about the three kinds of crazy that were generally recognized around Monacan.

The worst, he said, was "crazy as a bat." It came complete with private voices and overcoats in July and would earn a person full tuition at Central State Hospital.

The other two conditions, which didn't quite achieve the critical mass to cross the fine line between commitment and normalcy, were "not right" and "full of meanness."

"Not right," Carter instructed, implied a kind of passive lunacy whose practitioners posed more of a nuisance than a threat to those around them.

He told Nancy about Jeanette Faris' brother, Charles Royal, who had lived with Jeanette and her husband, Bob, for 14 years, in a back room up over their garage. He said Bob hadn't gotten a clear look at his brother-in-law for the last 12 years. They would just leave Charles' food by the door; he had his own bathroom. It didn't hurt anybody, and Jeanette told friends that Charles would come out after Bob went to work sometimes and talk to her, but nobody had seen him outside the house in 14 years. Carter said he and Marie used to visit Bob and Jeanette once in a while. They'd hear something go bump in the back room, and Jeanette might just kind of roll her eyes and they'd give her an understanding look. Marie added that the Royals were all a little peculiar, the unspoken other shoe being that all that "peculiar" is bound to spawn a little "not right" once in a while.

Most of those classified as "not right" tried to stay away from society in general as much as possible, Carter said. Those seen to be "full of meanness," though, were more aggressive, and it was society that did most of the avoiding.

"Like Uncle Lot," Sam said, and Carter didn't say anything.

Everybody in Monacan and the northern half of Mosby County seemed to know not to get Lot Chastain started. Carter said he'd seen him get into a fight with a man over whether you should use red pepper and Vaseline to keep snakes out of a bluebird house. Lot's argument was that if God meant for the snake to get the bluebirds, then it was His will and we shouldn't do anything to get in the way of His will.

In addition to the regular menu of religion, sex and politics, Lot Chastain was said to always have a blue-plate special or two boiling inside his brain, and the only way to find out what was cooking at any particular time was to talk to him, so Lot didn't have much company.

Before he became something of a celebrity, the last time anybody outside his family had seen him have one of his spells was in February. Carter was the one who told Nancy about it. He was the one who usually had to make things right.

Lot was at Wampler's Barber Shop, waiting to have his hair cut. A man who they said was from Wood's Store, who had brought his wife to Monacan to visit her aunt, was in the chair. Lot was second in line, drinking a Nehi strawberry soda, reading a back issue of Life.

Carter told Nancy that, the way it was related to him, the man from Wood's Store said he was thinking about buying one of "them Toyotas," and that from what he had heard, they were good little cars.

Lot looked up and smiled, but only with his mouth.

"That's that Jap car, isn't it?" he asked, in the quiet way he always seemed to start, the first small dark cloud presaging the storm.

Pen Graves, who was next in line, told Carter that he and John Wampler looked at each other, both of them hoping that the man from Wood's Store would just let it ride.

The man from Wood's Store didn't, though.

"Yeah, I reckon so," he said, giving the room in general a wink. "I reckon I can forgive 'em for World War II, though, if they'll give me a car that don't need a new transmission every 30,000 miles."

He was still chuckling to himself when Lot said, in a voice that had risen a decibel or two, "You wouldn't of thought it was so goddamn funny, I bet, if you'd of been on one of them islands out there in the Pacific, with them slant-eyed bastards waiting to skin you alive. That's what's wrong with this here country. We'd sell our mommas to make a dollar or two."

"I don't want to start nothin'," the man from Wood's Store said, and the other men in the barber shop saw his hands spread in a gesture of mollification under the striped sheet. "Hell, I was in the Army. I just want to buy a car."

"Don't want to start nothin'?" Lot was on cruise control now, just a missile that might land anywhere. "Don't want to start nothin'? Why, you dumb son of a bitch. Why you think we ain't speaking Japanese or German over here now? You think them bastards don't want to do it to us again? And we're helping them. God's going to punish us for not learning nothin'."

Lot Chastain was a big man to be 73 years old, a couple of inches over six feet, still rangy, not fat and not wasting away. He had long, hairy arms and long, bony fingers with gnarled knuckles. He had most of his hair, as much dark red as gray. When he got very angry, his face would turn purple in splotches where the blood seemed to gather, blocked there by the veins popping out in his neck. His eyes would go almost completely black and, if he was standing, his heels would leave the floor as if his rage were about to carry him away like a rocket.

The man from Wood's Store took offense, either to "dumb" or "son of a bitch," neither John Wampler nor Pen Graves was sure which.

He got out of the barber's chair, the sheet still around him. All he had a chance to get out was, "Now just a minute, old man. You can't call me . . ."

Lot jumped over the magazine table, spilling his strawberry soda all over his work shirt. He had his hands wrapped around the man from Wood's Store's neck before anybody could do anything about it. It took the other two men to pull him off.

By now, he had attracted a crowd, watching from a distance through the glass that separated John's barber shop from his father-in-law's grocery store. Minnie Turpin fainted when she saw the red splotch covering the front of Lot's shirt.

John Wampler called over his shoulder for somebody to get Carter while they tried to keep Lot from strangling the man from Wood's Store.

After they finally pulled him away, Lot continued to rant and rave.

"I was in the war, the big war, in 1917," he yelled at the man from Wood's Store, who was rubbing his neck and telling John Wampler that he was going to have Lot thrown in jail. "Them people want to kill us, and we're a-helping them!"

Carter ran there from his drugstore and somehow persuaded the man Lot had tried to choke not to press charges, told him in a quiet voice off to the side that Lot couldn't help it, that he just got like that sometimes. He gave the man $20 to buy a new shirt to replace the one that Lot had more or less ruined the collar of while trying to kill him. It was a tribute to Carter that Lot had never spent a night in jail.

The man from Wood's Store, with half a haircut and a ripped shirt, took the $20 and walked out through the crowd that had gathered outside. As he got to his car, he turned around and said to Carter, "I ain't planning to press charges, but you ought to do something about that old man. He's crazy."

Which, of course, started Lot off again. He lunged at the car and had to be pulled off the hood, by three men this time, taking the hood ornament with him.

In early May of 1971, Lot turned what a lot of people in Monacan thought was a corner.

Nobody had seen him for three days when Aileen, who was his and Carter's oldest sister, came out to visit him. She sometimes would take dinner, arriving unannounced, sure that whatever she'd left in the Crockpot before work that morning or picked up at the Barbecue Hut would be better than what Lot fixed for himself.

Coming into Monacan on the way home from her job in the shoe department at Thalhimer's, she passed the semicircular road on the left that led to the town itself, then took the right off Route 17 toward Old Monacan, her girlhood home. The pavement ran out after a mile, then the clay road turned into two ruts at the Jeters' driveway.

Simon Jeter's driveway was a sore point to the entire Chastain family, and to Lot in particular. You couldn't drive to Old Monacan, where Lot lived, without following the Jeter driveway through Jeter's barn, where the one-lane rut road was only sometimes blocked by a car.

The Chastains had used this road for two centuries, since the old Indian trail was turned into Route 17. It was their only link to the state highway that supplanted the river and eventually turned Old Monacan into a ghost town.

But then, in 1966, Simon Jeter, whom the Chastains had all known from when he was their tenant farmer, bought the 30 acres surrounding his cinder-block house, against Lot's wishes. The first thing Jeter did was build a new barn, to which he added a little shed that hung off the side farthest from his house. He built the shed, which had no walls, only a roof, so that it straddled the rut road to Old Monacan, which even then had a population of one. From then on, Lot Chastain had to drive through Simon Jeter's shed to go to and from his home.

Jeter said that he only wanted to use the covered, open-sided space for barning tobacco, so the help could sit in the shade while they tied the leaves onto sticks prior to hanging them in the barn. When he barned tobacco for the Chastains, he claimed that Lot's father made him and the rest of his family work out in the sun, telling them that they'd get lazy if they were allowed to sit in the shade.

The problem was, Jeter had no garage, and he started using the shed as a carport from time to time.

Aileen admitted that her brother didn't help things much. The first time that Jeter forgot and parked his car under the shed so that Lot couldn't get his old red Chevy pickup past, Lot just sat in the road and blew his horn until Jeter finally appeared, and then he cussed Jeter out for blocking him in. Jeter cussed him back, and they fought. Jeter was almost as old as Lot, and neither of them did much damage, but Lot used a different strategy from then on.

If he rounded the only curve coming from Old Monacan and saw Jeter's car blocking the road, he would just drive around the barn and shed, through Jeter's bean field, taking out as much vegatation as he could, blowing the horn as he went past. Jeter threatened to have him arrested, and Lot threatened to have Jeter arrested. Finally, a sheriff's deputy convinced Jeter that using a road for 200 years entitled you to keep on using it, but Jeter still forgot from time to time.

A Jeter grandchild, standing in front of one of the two trailers that now flanked the rut road, seemed to be waving at Aileen, holding back a stray sliver of lank brown hair with her free hand. Aileen started to wave back when she realized that the child, brown as a berry with the dusty look of all the Jeters, was extending her middle finger toward the car. She's probably used to doing that to anybody that comes back here, Aileen thought.

The road past Jeter's crossed a branch that would soon feed into a creek that, a mile away, expired into the river. Just beyond the branch was Old Monacan itself. Aileen drove past mounds that were the chimneys and rotting wood and general substance of houses abandoned as much as a century ago, overgrown with thorns and poison ivy. A snake suddenly slid into her field of vision. She floored the accelerator, but it disappeared into the green, car-high jungle on her right. She thought it looked like a pilot snake.

Slightly shaken, wishing she'd run it over, Aileen drifted into the sand bank and almost got stuck making the 90-degree left turn that came 100 yards before her final destination. She parked in front of Lot's trailer, behind his pickup. The mobile home itself was 10 years old and stood right in front of the old Chastain place; Lot had bought it and moved out of the big house after their mother died. Every two months, Aileen, Grace and Holly would come out on a Saturday to do what they could to keep the big house from falling in, then make Lot leave while they cleaned the trailer, although Grace was always saying she wasn't coming back after what Lot said to her the last time.

From there, on what used to be the second row of houses back from the water before the first row was eventually abandoned and finally caved in or burned down, Aileen could see the river. In the fading light, she could glimpse a flash from the C&O tracks on the other side and could barely make out the electric lights back in the shade that sheltered French Crossing.

The river here played a trick. Just before Old Monacan, it took a wild swing from its eastern course, doubling back toward the northwest. Where it doubled back, it pinched in so tight that a grown man could wade across it most days, the narrowness being the reason for Old Monacan's existence.

From the two-room Monacan public library, Nancy later learned this: Here, before they built the bridge downstream where the river righted itself and headed east again, Huguenot settlers who thought they were bound for the town craftsman's life they knew in France were left to learn how to farm and fight Indians, a buffer for the English to the east. The easy crossing had been used by the Monacan Indians since long before the oldest of them could remember, and the Huguenots seized it for their own, killing and dispersing the Monacans and stealing their name.

From the Huguenot town, farmers on the river's south side could transport their crops over to French Crossing, where the straightest, safest road east was.

A ferry and then a road five miles closer to Richmond began the transition of Monacan to Old Monacan, and the population went from 400 in 1850 to 40 a century later, by which time Monacan Courthouse, the county seat, had become just Monacan. The penultimate dwellers in the old town, the Dances, had left in 1962; their ruined house was the only standing structure left by 1971 other than the Chastain home, Lot's trailer, and the barn, if you didn't count a sawdust pile as a structure.

Aileen knocked on the trailer door and called a time or two for Lot, but she didn't hear anything except Lot's dog, Granger, growling somewhere out of sight. She thought of the snake, and chillbumps appeared on her arms. The old place didn't use to give her the willies, she thought, wondering if her nerves were going bad, like Holly's.

She decided to walk around the side of the trailer to where she could see the barn, and there Lot was, not seeming to pay any attention to anything except the gray-brown back of the building. Aileen's and Lot's father used to tell them why his father said he had built the barn with its backside to the house after he bought the land from a discouraged and departing former neighbor: "So's I can sit on my porch and not see anything to remind me of work."

The barn was turned a degree or two north of dead west and was catching the sun in that brief instant between its descent below the branches of the sycamores and its disappearance beyond the farmed-level horizon across the river. The back of it, where Lot stood, went long winter months without catching the sun at all. The sight of its illuminated surface on an April afternoon had been a sign of spring for four generations of Chastains, Aileen knew, counting her Stanley, Holly's girls, and Carter's boy. Maybe sometime soon Sam and his wife would let her take them out here so she could tell the story to their boy, and then it'd be five generations.

Aileen had come within ten feet of her older brother and was about to ask him if he had gone deaf when he spoke first.

"I want you to look at that," he told her, and his face had the purple splotches on it that usually just meant he was about to throw a fit.

Aileen looked at where he was staring, at the barn's side.

"What?" she asked him, and he looked at her for the first time.

"Can't you see it?" he asked her. "Can't you see the head up there, and the arms out here to the side? And the feet? Lookahere. There's even a nail there."

Aileen moved closer, squinting through her bifocals and staring at the bleached boards, where moss had gathered during the cold, dark fall and winter, until she could finally make out what he was pointing to.

And, she said later, she had to finally concede that what her brother had on the back side of his barn was a fairly believable rendition, done in moss and the vagaries in color that varying sunlight had caused over decades, of Our Lord Jesus Christ, up on the cross.

CHAPTER FIVE

In the four years she and Sam have been married, Nancy has been in the same room with Lot twice, both times the same day. It was Christmas two years past, just before Wade was born. They were in Old Monacan, at Sam's late grandparents' house. There were only two times of year that the house was used any more, Sam's father had told her: Christmas and the family Easter egg hunt.

Nancy watched Carter wedge the unused, wadded-up Christmas Day newspaper between the hearth and the grate, then place the oily fat lightning pine on top of the grate, finally putting on a few small split pieces of oak. The fat lightning ignited from the paper as if it held gasoline inside its nearly transparent shell, and soon the oak caught. Nancy was sitting as close to the hearth as she could, the two sides of her body many degrees apart in warmth, when Aileen heard tires on dirt and went to one of the big-paned windows with its imperfect glass.

"My lord," she said. "It's Lot."

The rest of the family went to the window. Lot was getting out of his old red Chevrolet pickup. Tufts of auburn hair hung out from the sides and back of an adjustable baseball cap. He was wearing work shoes, work pants, a tan work shirt and, for some reason, a blue tie.

Usually, Sam had already told her, Lot would go somewhere, nobody knew where, if the family was going to get together. He didn't mind a couple of his sisters coming out, or Carter, but he said he didn't like to be crowded.

Lot walked up the rotting steps to the front porch, and Holly, Sam's youngest aunt, opened the door slowly. Lot looked for a second as if he were going to hug her, but then he just walked in the door, squeezing her arm a little too hard as he went past.

Nancy, who had been looking out the window since the doorway was packed with full-blooded Chastains, saw a man whose eyes seemed to be pure black, making his attempt to smile appear more mocking than kind.

"I don't reckon you all expected to see me today," he said, in a high, nasal voice.

Although it seemed obvious that this was a rare visit, nobody ran forward to greet him right away. Rather, they approached him cautiously to shake hands or give him a hug or just to be introduced. It reminded Nancy of the way she and Marilou used to try to catch Pat's old Walker hound when he'd escape, fearful that a sudden move or loud noise might make him run beyond their grasp.

"Well, come on in and have some dinner," Aileen said.

Sam took Nancy's hand and led her over.

"Uncle Lot," he said, clearing his throat first, "this here is my wife. Nancy, this is my Uncle Lot," and Nancy thought to herself, "This here?"

Lot just stared at her at first, looking her up and down.

"Looks like you put on a little weight since I seen you in the wedding pictures," he said. Nancy looked up at her husband's uncle, who stood at least a foot taller.

"I hope to lose it soon," she said, angry at herself for blushing. And then she saw something in his expression that made her wonder if what she mistook for rough kidding about her pregnancy wasn't just a combination of rudeness and unawareness. But then everyone started scrambling to get dinner on the table, and she didn't have time to think about it.

The Chastains always ate before they opened the presents. Their first Christmas together, Nancy thought it strange that Sam felt obliged to buy something for all three of his aunts, his Uncle Lot, Grace and Holly's husbands, Aileen's son from New Jersey, Holly's daughters, Carlie and Zoe, who were in town from Washington and Charlotte, plus their children, plus Sam's father's first cousin, Pete Bondurant, who always had Christmas with the Chastains. But, the first Christmas they spent at the old Chastain place, she was glad she and Sam had bought everyone something, because everyone had bought them something. The tree was piled high with the token gifts of 18 people, most of them with gifts for the other 17. None of the presents they bought Sam's family cost more than $10, and Nancy tried not to notice that the ones they got back cost a good deal less than that: Whitman's Samplers and scarves and gift certificates at McDonald's.

As with the Christmas before, it took half the afternoon to open the gifts, with Aileen, Grace and Holly taking turns playing Santa Claus and everyone pretending that every gift was perfect, a treasure dreamed of for years. Nancy's face hurt.

Sometime in mid-afternoon, Lot started complaining that he wished everybody wouldn't make such a fuss about Christmas, that this wasn't what the baby Jesus had in mind, that it was a sin to spend this much. He was feeling bad, Nancy thought, because he didn't get anyone any gifts and they'd all brought him something for when he came home later. But when Holly gently suggested what Nancy had been thinking, Lot's face reddened, and he got up and stomped out the door before anyone could stop him.

"He's just having one of his spells," Aileen said in the silence he left in his wake, and Grace sighed.

But then, half an hour later, while Grace's husband Walter was showing Zoe how to crack walnuts with her hands, and Sam's aunts, who everyone referred to collectively as "the girls," were gathering used wrapping paper, saving the bows, Lot came back, his hair more askew than it had been before. His nails were dirty, and his sleeves, as if he'd been digging.

He walked over to Cole McMeans, Grace's husband, put something in his hand, and said, "Merry Christmas, Cole." Cole, a balding, slight man who seemed uncomfortable among the Chastains, mumbled a thank-you.

"I might be poor, but I might not be as poor as you all think," he said, amid protests.

He handed something to Zoe, something shiny. She thanked him, but he'd already gone on to Carter.

When he got near her, Nancy saw that he was giving away silver dollars. He had a small bag full of them, and when he got to her, he gave her two.

"I reckon you think I didn't know you was expectin'," he

said, with that same half-mocking smile. "That's one for each of you. And bring him to see me when he's born."

"Thank you," Nancy said. "I will."

"She's got good manners," Lot said, turning to Sam, "for a Richmond girl."

He finished his rounds, giving what was left to Carlie's and Zoe's children, who were trying to hide behind their mothers.

"Go on, I ain't a-going to hurt you," he said roughly, and he finally got them to take three each of the silver coins. Then, without speaking again, he was gone.

It was almost dark when Sam and Nancy left, promising everyone they'd come visit soon, Nancy hoping it would be Easter at least. As they walked to their car, Nancy's eyes burned from the slow, constant smoke of the sawdust pile, which had already smoldered three years and would smolder almost three more. They were even with the mobile home when they heard the trailer door slam. It was Lot, coming out with two cans of dog food, headed for the tree behind the house where he kept Granger tied up.

"You all leaving already?" he asked them. "The fun's just beginning."

"I reckon we better," Sam told him, and Nancy noticed again how his speech patterns seemed to change. He spoke in a more clipped style, all the g's enunciated, when he was in the city, but out here with his family, he fell into the softer cadence of the country.

"Well, come on in for a minute," he said with such urgency that Sam looked at Nancy, who shrugged, miffed that he was putting her in the position of snubbing someone in his family.

He set the dog food down at the edge of the cinder-block steps leading up to the trailer door, and they followed him in.

The air inside had the indefinable quality that Nancy always associated with Sam's family, some aroma of stale-bread turkey stuffing or buttermilk biscuits in it. A TV was carrying a pro football playoff game in the background, sitting on an older TV that apparently didn't work any more. The furniture seemed to have come with the trailer.

They sat down on the couch, barely wide enough for two, and he took the only chair in the cramped living room.

"I'm glad to see you all populating the earth," Lot said.

"Be fruitful and multiply. I never did get married. Never found the right girl, I reckon."

There wasn't much to say to that, Nancy thought.

He didn't offer anything to drink, and after a while he started watching TV. Sam was genuinely interested in the game, but after about five minutes, Lot started snoring.

"Come on," Sam whispered. Nancy followed him, wondering what the old man would think when he woke up and found his trailer empty.

"He won't remember a thing," Sam said, reading her mind as they stepped off the bottom step to the ground and she resisted the urge to sneeze as the smell of burning sawdust hit her again.

"What about his dog?" Nancy asked, looking over at the opened cans.

"Screw the dog," Sam said. "He's tried to bite me two times. Let's go."

She didn't think until later to ask Sam where Lot had gone, when he came back with all the silver dollars. She'd noticed at the time that his red truck didn't move from the front of the house.

"Nobody knows where Uncle Lot goes, or what he does," Sam said. "I don't think anybody wants to know."

Now it's two weeks after Sam told Nancy they were moving to Monacan. Living with Sam's parents while they decide whether to rent or buy has meant sacrificing a lot of privacy, but he keeps telling her that it won't be much longer. They've looked at several homes for sale around Monacan, although it is becoming obvious to Nancy that what Sam really wants to do is build on the vacant lot one street back from the one where he was raised. They agree to rent a house on the same street until they, meaning he, Nancy thinks, can decide.

Nancy still can't understand why she didn't just refuse to budge from their brick home on the North Side, just, as Suzanne suggested, "clear out a place on the floor and throw a shit-fit." Her family is more than a little hurt, although she alternately tells them it isn't permanent and that they'll visit every week, no matter what. They haven't seen Sam since the move. Monacan's not so bad, Nancy thinks half the time. It's not too late, she thinks the other half.

Sam makes his resignation from DrugLand official, and his father is in the process of having the papers drawn up to give Sam 50 percent of the Monacan Drug Store. Carter is almost 69, and Nancy can't help but think that this was a done deal before she ever met Sam.

The Monacan Drug Store is a treat, she has to admit. When she first visited here, when she and Sam were dating, she was taken by how much better Carter's working conditions were than those of his son. The Monacan Drug Store is in a two-story frame building that was the post office for a century. The second floor, reached by an outdoor stairway and surrounded by a spindle-railed porch, is taken up by Monacan Realty. The first level is Carter's. His drug store has a lunch counter running 25 feet down the left side as you walk in, so that the customers and Trudy French, behind the counter, can see everything that happens on Monacan's main street out the front or side windows with just a slight twist of their heads. Trudy makes milk shakes and limeade in addition to burgers, hot dogs and breakfast.

Carter Chastain is stationed at the back of the store, on a high stool behind smoky glass. He has a clerk to keep the shelves stocked and help the customers. The Monacan Drug Store is open 8–6, Monday through Friday, 8–12 on Saturdays, closed Sundays and national holidays.

What Monacan doesn't have, Nancy soon finds out, is a decent grocery store. She's trying to help Marie with the cooking, and she wants to fix Suzanne's chicken tarragon for Saturday night dinner the first week they're living in the big, red-brick house. She soon discovers that the Red Top Market, on courthouse square, doesn't have tarragon, shallots or white wine, so she leaves Wade with his grandmother and heads for the Giant in Westover, the closest grocery she can get to that doesn't depress her.

When she pulls the Duster into the lot, she sees that it is almost full of Friday evening shoppers. She loops around to the third, back row and finds a place near the end. She has the key out of the ignition and is opening the door when she sees a familiar red pickup on the second row, between her and the front door. It's after 7 and the light is fading, but she knows it's Lot. She also knows that any route she takes to the front door of the grocery store will take her close enough to him and his truck to make her uncomfortable. He doesn't seem to be going in. Maybe he's waiting for someone, but Nancy doesn't think so.

Finally, feeling foolish and a little mean-spirited, she turns on the ignition, drives out the exit, circles the building and enters the parking lot on the other side, parking even farther away. The only glance Lot could get of her from here, she knows, is when she rounds the corner to go in the front door.

Inside, with the sky almost given over to night at last, she sneaks a glance through the plate glass. The truck is still there, and she can see his silhouette. She takes her time shopping, and when she comes out, the truck is gone. She makes a mental note to go to the Ukrop's, five miles farther away, the next time.

CHAPTER SIX

I want you to look at them. Hanging around this parking lot, hooking up with each other to do who knows what later on.

That gal over there, looks like she might not be more'n 14, her head stuck inside that car window a-talking to them two boys, showing her tail to anybody that wants to look at it, probably fixing to go off somewheres with them and do it, maybe with both of 'em.

And that grown woman standing there, flirting with that bag boy, who looks like he ain't hardly old enough to be her son. What you reckon she's got on her filthy mind? Not wearing nothing but one of them mini-skirts that Carter says ain't no harm, they just wear them to play tennis, but I know better. You can see near-bout everything she's got.

And them two colored folks in the truck up in front, her sitting right next to him like they was at the Riverview watching the X-rated drive-in movies or something. Been riding around town like that, I reckon, her probably playing with his thing. He gives her a big, long kiss before they get out to go inside. Just asking the Lord to rain down brimstone on them.

I remember how disgusted Momma used to act when we'd be a-looking at the soap operas on TV, how everybody seemed like they was going to bed with everybody else. And it's even worse now. It embarrassed me to death that she wanted to look at that stuff, but she never hardly missed a day until they took her to the hospital the last time.

And them magazines. I had to fuss with Johnny Wampler at the barber shop because of the filth he lets get in there. He had that there Sports Illustrated *with all them girls in swimming suits where they might as well not of had anything on at all. Any young'un coming in for a haircut could just pick it up and look at it. And Johnny said he didn't see no harm in it, that that wasn't nothing compared to what they show in* Playboy *and them others.*

*I know. I had to get after Carter to quit carrying them magazines
in the drug store, told him how ashamed Momma and Daddy would
be of him, how they can still see him, up in heaven. And he did
finally throw that filth out. Reckon he got tired of fussing about it.*

*You can see about anything you want, right here in the parking
lot. Like that city girl Carter's boy married. She thinks I didn't see
her when she turned in, then just sat there for a while, but I don't
miss much. I spied her in my rearview mirror, cruising by in that
Plymouth automobile of theirs, not a sign of Carter's boy or their
baby. Looked like she was a-waitin' for somebody, then just drove off
real quiet, circled around and come in the other side. Maybe she seen
her boyfriend parked over on that side. Can't trust none of them.
Momma was right. Just want to get you to work yourself to death
so they can slip out and do it.*

*Had that fat lightning dream again, except now I'm at the table
with all the family there. Don't know what they're eating, but I'm
chewing on that fat lightning like it was ham. And don't nobody say
anything or notice anything until Sam's wife starts staring at me,
and then everybody does, and then they all start a-laughing, her
louder than the rest, that trashy city laugh of hers.*

*And then I see Sam's wife slip around the corner and go in the
front door of the Giant, giving a little glance over her shoulder like
she knows she's been spied. Reckon maybe she'll pick up some milk
for the baby and then go back to her van or his car and kiss some
more. Maybe they'll just do it right there in the lot, with it not even
dark yet. Maybe she'll just take off her panties and spread her legs
like some whore right there in the van where if Sam was smart he'd
even get a whiff of it when they was driving to church Sunday
morning. Just do it right there where anybody could see 'em, and
her not caring a-tall. Just do it. Do it. Do it. Do it. Do it.*

CHAPTER SEVEN

By the middle of May, Sam and Nancy have put their home in Richmond up for sale and moved into the Fischer place, a block back and two houses over from Sam's parents. Mrs. Fischer died a year ago, and her children, scattered throughout the state, are willing to rent with an option to buy.

It's not an old house, by Monacan standards, built in the first 20 years of the century, with a nook carved into the wall where the telephone was put in later, arched doorways and ornate trimwork. The outside is old brick, like most of the houses in Monacan. There's a basement with a washer and room for a dryer, a garage full of old magazines and bottles that even the Fischer children didn't want, a front porch and a back porch. The back yard even has a chain-link fence so that Nancy can turn Wade loose for a few minutes while she tries to write.

Nancy is still thinking of all this as a temporary move, or temporary insanity. When she sits in her family's comfortable house on Richmond's North Side or she and Marilou and Candy get away and spend the evening in the Fan's high-ceilinged restaurants and bars, she thinks that she can't devote the rest of her life to a town where you have to import green peppercorns.

She's read a history of Mosby County that she found while browsing in Monacan's cramped library, half the size of Sam's father's drugstore, only open 10 to 4, Monday through Friday. From reading this book, Nancy's main impression of Old Monacan, where Lot lives, is that it is prone to have a disaster every 100 years.

In 1678, it was the Indians massacring the Huguenots, killing dozens and scattering the rest before the militia came back to kill every Indian found in a 10-mile radius.

In 1773, a flood destroyed most of the town, persuading the settlers to rebuild farther back from the river.

In 1879, a fire burned up four blocks; it was already losing dominance to the new town on the main road, two miles away.

Nancy likes the permanent feel of Monacan itself. There are sidewalks old enough to be cracking from maple and willow roots coming up underneath, and the houses in the town's six residential blocks are all solidly brick and well-shaded, so that she can pretend she's back in the tamer streets of Richmond if she doesn't look to the ends of these streets where corn and tobacco back up to side yards.

Nancy and Sam are watching TV, enjoying the hour or so between the time Wade goes down and they themselves do the same, when the old doorbell gives a muted ring.

"Well, hey, Aunt Aileen," Nancy hears Sam say, and she knows their short evening break is over. She switches off the TV.

"Now, don't turn that thing off on my account," Aileen says. "I can't stay anyhow."

But Nancy does get her to stay. Aileen talks about Grace's hiatal hernia and Holly's daughter Zoe, who doesn't visit enough, and finally works her way around to the business she came for, in the roundabout way Nancy has noticed is a trademark of Sam's family. Either they just blurt it out, or they dance around it so long you wish they would just blurt it out.

Finally, she says, "Sam, I think Lot might be losing his mind."

"Well, how can you tell, Aunt Aileen?" Sam says. Nancy laughs, thinking Sam's making a joke, then sees that this is an inappropriate response.

So, Aileen tells them about the barn door, where Lot showed her the image of Jesus.

"He says it's there every day, right before sunset," Aileen says. "I don't know who's going to look after him if he loses his mind. I can't bear the thought of having to lock him up."

"Aw, Aunt Aileen, he'll be OK. He's always been excitable," Sam says. "He'll outlive us all." This last is the first part of a family joke of sorts. The unspoken punch line is, "He'll aggravate the rest of us to death first."

"The worst part," she says, "is that, when I looked at that barn, and looked where he told me to, it was like I could see Jesus on the cross. Do you reckon I'm losing my mind, too?"

"It's like clouds," Nancy says, and from the looks both of them give her, she immediately feels she's cut in on a private conversation. "You know, you look up at a cloud and you can see just about anything you want to see."

She's embarrassed and then infuriated when not only Aileen but also Sam stare at her as if SHE's lost her mind.

"I'll make some coffee," she says.

Later, in bed, Sam tells her that Aileen said she saw the image two weeks ago, but that she didn't want to tell anybody because she was afraid people would think the whole family was crazy.

"We're going out there tomorrow evening," Sam says. "You promised Uncle Lot you'd let him see Wade anyhow."

"When?"

"Christmas. Two years ago."

"Before he was born? You remember plenty when you want to. You couldn't remember the times we lay in the grass at Byrd Park and made up stories about clouds, though, could you?"

Sam does a quarter-turn to face her in the dark. "There wasn't any sense in changing the subject, was there?"

Nancy doesn't say anything, but she realizes, lying in the dark, that she is more angry with Sam about this than about his moving them to Monacan.

She's been lying on her side, away from Sam, for perhaps five minutes, too upset to sleep, when she hears a small voice:

"Am I being lamb-blasted?"

She tries to stay mad at him, but the memory makes her start giggling.

"Goddammit, Sam, let me stay mad," she says, rolling over and punching him in the ribs.

"Just don't lamb-blast me," he says, pulling the pillow over his head with both hands in anticipation of the attack that usually leads to some rather fierce love-making.

When they were not yet married and were renting an apartment on a not-yet-gentrified street in the Fan, they had a landlord who lived in the unit above theirs and fought constantly with his wife.

Once, after Sam and Nancy had spent a sleepless hour listening to a dish-throwing argument that began when Mr. Loughery came in around 2 a.m. one Sunday, they ran into their landlord on their way to brunch.

He was sitting on the front stoop, staring at a similar stoop across the street. He had on what appeared to be the same clothes he'd worn when he tried to slip home unnoticed a few hours earlier. He hadn't shaved, and his hands were locked behind his head, seemingly to keep it from falling off and rolling down the steps into the street.

Mr. Loughery looked up at them with bloodshot eyes.

"She fwowed me out," he said. Mr. Loughery usually pronounced "th" sounds as "f," and his "r's" sometimes sounded like "w's."

"I'm fwew wif her," he said. "She's all the time lamb-blasting me."

For years, Sam could defuse any argument by accusing Nancy of "lamb-blasting" him, and she realizes now that he hasn't used their old code word in six months at least, that what arguments they have show a disturbing tendency not to dissipate but to harden into cold little lumps, out of sight but only out of mind until the next disagreement. Sam, who was always quiet, just seems to pull the flaps of his tent closed now rather than deal with unpleasantness.

Nancy, lying now facing her husband, who's fallen into a post-coital sleep and is snoring lightly, misses the humor.

The next day is a Wednesday. Sam is home by 6:10; he hasn't failed yet to mention how he can walk from his father's drugstore, soon to be his, more quickly than he could drive from the DrugLand to their home in Richmond.

Nancy has made spaghetti. They eat, with Nancy mashing up little bits for Wade, and then, as they are finishing dinner, Aileen pulls into the circular drive.

"Is it really necessary for me to go?" Nancy asks.

"I think his feelings would be hurt if you didn't bring Wade along."

"Well, you take him then. Your uncle doesn't care about seeing me."

Sam gives her his hurt look, and she sighs, then goes to get a wet cloth to wipe off Wade's sauce-encrusted face while Sam answers the front door.

On the way over, nobody says much. The land from Route 17 to Old Monacan has a gouged-out appearance. The Jeters have sold off trees on much of their property, and the bare patches expose a clay so red it makes Nancy uneasy, a red that can be detected on a moonlit night. She's noticed it in the clothes of workmen in the area, a dark stain that doesn't seem to ever go away. But as they come around the curve that marks the boundary between Jeter's land and the old Chastain property, the old oaks, sycamores and willows are preserved. The rest of the family would prefer that Lot did sell some of his timber, but he's made it clear to them that not one limb of his mother's and father's trees will be hauled off by the lumber men as long as he lives.

It's 7:30 by the time they get there, and the sun is almost low enough to shine beneath the branches of the sycamore west of the barn. It seems to be a deeper orange here than in the city, Nancy thinks, probably because of the smoke from the sawdust pile. She will forever associate this place with a smoldering, almost-ignited scent. The sky's few clouds are turning pink, and a jet contrail forms a straight line high above them.

Sam parks the car beside Lot's trailer and goes around to open the front passenger door for Aileen while Nancy helps Wade out of the car seat. Lot himself comes walking toward them, from the barn. He's not alone. Behind him, keeping a distance, are two boys who seem to be about 14 years old.

"You all like to have missed it," he says. "Come on."

They walk back toward the barn, which Sam has told Nancy is built over the ruins of an early settler's abandoned home. The sun is hitting the barn straight on now; in 15 minutes it will disappear.

"The one with the red hair is a Jeter," Lot says to his visitors. "The other one is a Basset."

Wade has his head on Nancy's shoulder, with his thumb in his mouth, ready to go to sleep, when Lot notices him.

"Come here, boy," he says with an unpracticed mock

roughness that Wade misinterprets. He starts to cry when Lot tries to hold him.

"I reckon he's just backward, is all," Lot says and turns away. By now, everyone is looking at the barn, no one saying a word. Finally, Lot starts pointing out where the arms and legs, even the nails, are.

"Up there, see the crown of thorns?" he says, pointing several slats up from eye level.

Sam and Nancy both have to admit to themselves, later, that it is an amazing likeness of Jesus on the cross. Somehow, the mold and aging have given the boards a design. And, unlike the clouds, it doesn't seem to change.

"That's amazing, Uncle Lot," Sam says.

"Have you ever seen anything like it?" Aileen says, and Nancy shakes her head. Lot has a proud, proprietary look.

The two boys have been helping Lot clear his garden.

"Granddaddy'd beat me good if he knew I come over here," the red-headed one, the Jeter, says. The other boy, who has deeply tanned skin and sandy hair, says nothing, but he can't keep his eyes off the side of the barn, staring for five minutes after it's impossible to see anything in the fading light.

"Do you reckon we're all crazy?" Aileen asks no one in particular.

"They thought Jesus was crazy, too," Lot says.

By now, they're walking back toward the trailer, past the side of the big house. The Jeter boy has headed off through the woods home, but the Basset is staying, hanging back a few steps.

"He's got him a tent over there," Lot motions with his head toward the river to their left. "He's from French Crossing, and his folks don't give him much showing, so sometimes he just wades across, or takes the jonboat if the water's high. Don't hurt nothing."

Lot speaks to Nancy individually for the first time since they got there.

"I don't reckon you all got anything like this back in Richmond," he says.

"I don't guess so," she says. She's tired by now of carrying Wade. Sam takes the child from her.

"He looks kind of like Daddy," Lot says, and everybody

51

nods their heads. "Wish you all would of come before he got so cranky."

Nancy looks at Sam, who wills her not to snap back at the old man. They talk awhile, then decline Lot's invitation to come inside. By 9:30, they're back in Monacan, which seems like a city to Nancy after Old Monacan. Aileen doesn't come in. Before she drives off, she asks, "Do you reckon we ought to tell anybody about this, Sam?" and Sam shrugs his shoulders. "Don't suppose it'd hurt anything, Aunt Aileen."

Nancy puts Wade to bed. She still doesn't know what to think about what they've seen, but she wonders if there isn't a short story, or even another novel—one that won't return—in her husband's uncle. If, she thinks to herself, anybody could stand to be around him long enough.

CHAPTER EIGHT

Steed Jackson, the editor of the Herald, hears about Lot's barn and comes out with his camera one weekday afternoon in early June. The image doesn't photograph well at all, but the Herald story alerts everyone in the county who hasn't heard about it yet by word of mouth. The Times-Dispatch sends a reporter out from Richmond, and they do a story on it that is read all over the state. Then The Associated Press picks it up and does a rewrite referring to the people in and around Monacan as "folks." Lot begins getting calls from radio and TV stations in other states.

Soon, the road that goes through Simon Jeter's barn, the road that can go for days without any traffic, is congested. People coming and going on the rut trail beyond the barn have to take to the fields to avoid colliding with each other. By mid-June, it is not unusual for 100 people to be standing at the barn by 8 p.m., waiting for the sun's rays to hit the right spot.

"There! I can see his feet!" one old man might say. "There's the crown of thorns!" a woman holding a Bible might add, pointing with her free hand. Slowly, the crowd verbally puts together the puzzle on the side of Lot's barn, a low murmur and occasional shout breaking the silence. They stand and watch until the sun's last light has faded, then they silently go back to their cars, which are parked all around the old Chastain house and down the rut road that goes by Lot's trailer.

Lot himself usually stands back from the crowd, accepting the occasional compliment from shy pilgrims as his rightful due.

"The Lord is trying to tell us something," he might say,

and two or three people in the background will murmur, "Amen." He's still surprised that, for the first time in his life, people seem to move closer when he starts expressing his opinions rather than try to find an exit. Most of the people aren't from around Monacan. The locals all saw it the first two weeks after Aileen spread the word. Other than occasional family members and the Basset boy, most of the people who come now are from other parts of the county, and some come from as far away as Richmond or Lynchburg. He's surprised that Sam's wife has come back twice. He always gets her name mixed up, because she looks a little like Holly used to. He doesn't trust her, and he suspects that she's laughing at him behind his back, but he always tries to be sociable.

Jeter's grandson has stopped coming, and word gets out that he's run away. He's done that twice before, so nobody other than the Jeters themselves seems too worried about it.

When Lot realizes that people actually want to hear what he has to say about things, he's ready to oblige, realizes that he's been waiting all his life for this. Some people think he's shy, but he's just doing what his mother advised him to do, when he had not yet quit school and he'd get in fights every day, other children calling him "crazy" and "vacant Lot."

"Sugar," she told him, looking at him with those same nearly black eyes, her hand on his arm, "they're just jealous because you know so much. But you got to keep it inside, otherwise they'll make up stuff and put you in Central State just for spite. You know what you know. Don't have to tell it to nobody."

Lot has never forgotten this. He tries not to let all the world's sin get to him, because when it does, he winds up embarrassing his family. He's lived at home for 71 of his 73 years, working as a carpenter here and there and helping his father farm from the time he got back from World War I until his father died. He never went to church, even though almost everyone who used to talk about him behind his back before the war was gone now. He and his mother got along much better after his father died, because the two men would always get into arguments, sometimes threatening to kill each other.

But now, when he clears his throat, these people, some of

them wearing fresh dresses and coats and ties like they were going to church, get quiet. And Lot finds that he has a lifetime of things to say.

"He's a-coming back," he says to his audience. "This here's a sign; I know it is. He's coming to pay us back for all this wickedness, all this here free sex and burnin' the flag and all. You think we couldn't beat them Viet Congs if we wasn't being punished by God?"

And sometimes Lot will throw in a verse from Revelation, which he has always read, more times than he can remember.

"'And the temple was filled with smoke from the glory of God, and from his power,'" Lot will read, "'and no man was able to enter into the temple, till the seven plagues of the seven angels were fulfilled.'" Lot can find most of what he wants to find in Revelation with a quick flip of his thumb through the worn pages. His Bible looks like a book that someone has started reading from the wrong end: dog-eared at the back instead of the front.

Sometimes, when Lot reads, the wind will shift and blow in the strong scent of the burning sawdust pile from the south, causing people to take out handkerchiefs to wipe their eyes and blow their noses, giving a muffled air to the "Amens."

Billy Basset is usually among the crowd. He's never seen anything like the image on the barn, and being there, along with the now-departed Terry Jeter, right from the beginning gives him a feeling of importance he's not used to. Now, with school out, he doesn't have anywhere better to go than the old home he's always looked at from across the river, that looks smaller and more run-down than he'd always imagined it.

But Billy isn't camping out in the yard any more. A week after the old man let him stay the first time, he started slipping into the old house at night. He found that two of the beds still had mattresses, and he even found an old alarm clock, so he could get up and go back out to the tent before sunrise.

He has also found that the old Chastain house has many items worth stealing. Billy has been a petty thief since he was 12. He finances his clothes and spending money by stealing and dealing drugs. His distributor, a retired Richmond city policeman who lives on the state road south of Monacan, can also sell just about any of the hot merchandise Billy brings him.

Billy is smart enough to take small things from out-of-the-way places, things that won't be missed. He's discovered a cubbyhole behind a wall that contains many of what his distributor calls antiques: old jewelry boxes, some minor jewelry, a pair of candelabras, dolls. One happy night Billy finds, rummaging around with his flashlight, a box full of silver dinnerware. About once a week, he goes on one of his scavenger hunts. Then he slips what he considers to be valuable out to his jonboat and goes back across the river the next morning. From there, he can get a ride to Monacan.

Billy is also smart enough to convince Lot that he's camping at the Chastain place for religious reasons. His grandmother has beaten enough of the Bible into him, Old and New Testaments, that he can talk a good game. His grandmother, like Lot, was especially fond of Revelation.

Lot likes to ask Billy questions about Revelation, such as, "How many elders in the fourth chapter?" And Billy can often give him the correct answer. When he does, Lot nods his head and might launch into a monologue about the end of the world. When Billy answers incorrectly or says he doesn't know, Lot makes him read the passage that gives the correct answer. Billy is a fast learner.

He's even got Granger, Lot's half-chow, half-German shepherd, on his side. When Billy sneaks out of the house in the dark, sometimes loaded with family relics, he can speak a quiet word and the dog stays silent.

By mid-June, the occasional out-of-state car arrives.

A woman from Steubenville, Ohio, prematurely gray, comes up one afternoon in a Ford Torino the color of her hair. She says she's driven since early morning, that she heard of the miracle of the barn on an all-night religious talk show on the radio. She waited until her husband came in from the graveyard shift and went to bed, then got his keys and headed south. She stays for two days, sleeping in her car, until Lot calls the sheriff's department and then her husband comes for her.

A couple from Iowa, driving a Winnebago across the country at the start of the husband's retirement, find their way to Old Monacan, managing to get stuck twice within 200 yards of Lot's trailer.

A black man from Tabor City, North Carolina, appears one evening, just as the sun is about to hit the side of the barn. He has no car; he's walked all the way from Monacan, where he got off the bus. He says he wants to see the picture of Jesus. He stands with the mostly white crowd for 45 minutes, then turns and walks away, never to be seen again.

The sheriff has dispatched a deputy by now for crowd control, but there isn't much he can do. The Chastain home has one small drive that fans out at what was the family garage, and the only thing for the pilgrims to do is park on the side of the rut road or in the edge of the bean field. The daily traffic has widened the trail from Jeter's to Lot's trailer so that now two cars can pass on it, but it usually takes an hour to clear everybody out after the sun sets.

Nancy comes back once a week, despite Lot. She tries to mingle with the others, but he always spots her and tries to get her to come over to his trailer for a visit.

She takes a notebook with her and tries, as unobtrusively as she can, to get it all down on paper. She's put her first novel, the homing novel, on the shelf, and she thinks she can use Lot and his barn as background for a second one. Sam is already gently pressuring her to take over as cashier at the drugstore, telling her that his mother will be glad to take care of Wade during the day, but she keeps putting him off. She fears that this somehow would be the final capitulation, that it would seal her fate forever. Sam, since the forced move from Richmond, has been less demanding than usual, and Nancy intends to stay out of the family business as long as possible.

She goes out to Old Monacan on Wednesday evenings, when Sam goes to his Civitan meeting, something he says he has to do as a businessman, something Nancy knows he'd never have done five years ago. She leaves the baby with Sam's parents, telling them she's going for a drive. They and Sam know she has been back out to Lot's, but for now they're not asking any questions.

The third time she goes out to Old Monacan by herself, the old man asks her again to stay and have some iced tea. She has no intention of going inside with him, but to hide her general uneasiness, she asks him about the burning sawdust pile. She's heard that there was another one, many years ago. Lot tells her as much as he wants to tell her, about how the present pile has been there since the sawmill went broke in the Depression, taking the place of an earlier one that eventually smoldered down to nothing.

By the time he's through, the last few stragglers have an open road in front of them.

CHAPTER NINE

Fire chief's been coming around here again. Wanted to know what I'm fixing to do about the sawdust pile. Told him, not a blessed thing. That sawdust pile ain't hurting a soul; just let it smoke. It'll burn itself out. He said it was a hazard, and I said, to what? Do I look like I'm crazy enough to climb up on top of it? Who's going to care if I do? Are you fretting about my dog? Even he's got sense enough not to walk on top of something that's a-smokin' all the time. Even Granger knows there's a fire 'way down under there. Ain't nobody else got any business over by it.

So then the fire chief says, but what about all them people that comes out here to look at that picture of Jesus on the side of your barn? And I tell him, first, it ain't no picture, it's a vision, and, second, there's a No Trespassing sign right back of the barn, and nobody wants to have nothing to do with that sawdust pile anyhow.

Seems like them folks from Richmond and Norfolk and all is scared of it. And when the wind changes, you ought to see 'em start blowing their noses and rubbing their eyes when them cinders start to fly. Ought to get a fan and put it on the other side so I could clear 'em out when I'm tired of all of 'em hanging around.

Shoot. Everybody's so fired up about my sawdust pile, like they think that's the worst thing they got to fret about. Like that's what's causing all them boys to get sent home in body bags. Like that's what makes white folks act so hateful towards the colored. Like that's what makes the well water go bad over around the county dump.

They just got to have somebody to mess with, and they think it's going to be me. People always been messing with me. They did it when I was a young'un. Sometimes I'd get so mad I'd just start a-hitting and then it'd go black and they'd tell me about it later, or sometimes they wouldn't. And back then, before the war, I had Warren to take up for me.

One time, we had this stray mutt that took up here, part beagle, part God knows what. Us boys was playing in the woods one day, and the dog followed me and Warren. Frankie Tubbs that lived in the house that burnt down back in '61 got hold of some gasoline from somewheres, so we could watch stuff burn.

First thing I knowed, Frankie had poured gasoline on that old liver-spotted mutt, and then he throwed a match on him. The dog run in circles so fast it just seemed like a hoop of fire, and then he run off. We didn't find the dog's body until the buzzards started circling. Frankie thought it was the funniest thing he ever seen. If Warren hadn't of pulled me off of him, he told me later, he reckoned I'd of killed him. And then they said I was the crazy one.

People think because I live out here by myself and ain't got no friends in high places and such that they can just mess with me when they feel like it. Like they're a-saying, here's the big criminal that's letting his sawdust pile burn. I bet the fire chief and all his big friends just laugh and laugh when they talk about what a hard time they're a-giving old Lot Chastain. Well, it'll keep on burning 'til it burns itself out. That's the way Daddy done it.

The other pile, the one that was between the one burning now and the river, it burnt most of the time I was a young'un, it seems like. Most of my recollections of this place has that burning wood smell in the back of it. And one day, it just caved in on its own when it had burnt enough, while I was off to war, after Holly left, too.

I remember we used to play over behind it, and we'd make like that sawdust pile was hell. Momma'd tell us if we didn't straighten up, the devil'd come out of there and get us and take us back down with him. Even had us believing it 'til we was old enough to know better.

And us boys would play a game Warren made up, called Tempt the Devil, where we'd all draw straws, and the one that got the short one would have to run right across the top of that smoking sawdust pile or be called a scairdy-cat. Then, the first one he tagged would have to come across, too. We'd get up at least six or seven young'uns, and nobody had to do it twice. We'd have to wait 'til it was near-bout dark, so's our folks wouldn't see us and give us a whipping.

Momma could be right mean unless you knew her like I did. She'd always tell me, "Lot, you're just like me. When you know a thing, you know it. You don't take no junk from nobody." She used to give Daddy a hard time.

Holly used to wouldn't go nowhere near that other sawdust pile unless I was with her. Wanted me to hold her hand when we walked past it. She liked to hang around with me when I'd go down to the river and fish. It was just her and me back then, me already 18 and her 10 or 11, although it didn't seem that much difference. But then folks got hateful and said things to her about me, and then I had to go into the Army, even though Warren was already gone and they ought to of let me stay and take care of Momma and Daddy, and when I come home, she was living with the Bondurants. Other folks is always doing something to see if they can't keep others from being too happy.

But this here's my sawdust pile now, and I kind of like the smell it gives off. So I tell the fire chief, who ain't nothing but the boss of a bunch of rascals that probably start most of the fires theirselves anyhow, that he ought to mind his own business and get off my property before I unleash Granger, who's already growling over there. He goes, but he tells me I got to do something about that fire.

My Lord. It's like that place outside of Richmond where Grace and Walter live. They can't cut a tree down or paint the house without some committee or commission or something telling them they can do it. Can't even pick out their own mailboxes, 'cause they all got to look alike. And if one of 'em buys a boat or a camper, they got to put it in a big lot two miles away, so it won't spoil the looks of the place sitting there in the driveway. Might as well be in Russia.

That's why I like to live right here. I know the rules here, 'cause they're the same ones Momma and Daddy had, and if anybody makes up any new ones, it's a-gonna be me. You live by my law here. That's what I ought to of told that Jeter boy, when I caught him.

CHAPTER TEN

Kim Stallings, who is on the Dabney High Class of '61 10-year reunion committee, tells Nancy that Buddy has sent in his $20.

"That's $20, Nance," she says. "The cost is $20 a person. If you bring a date, it's an extra $20. Wonder if Buddy's bringing anyone? Well, you do the math."

Sam isn't going. He'd just be bored, he tells her. She knows he's never been that close to any of her old friends.

Nancy goes with Sandy Hall Burden, her best friend from high school, and Sandy's husband, who was a year ahead of them. Sandy used to be known as Sandra, but when she went off to college at Old Dominion, she made everyone start calling her Sandy. Sandy's husband used to be known as Elbert, but he told everyone, as soon as he got out of high school, that he would be called Skip from then on. To Nancy's knowledge, no one had ever called him Skip before then. She still forgets sometimes. The three of them and Buddy used to double-date.

The reunion is the 22nd of June, a time of year when Richmond can feel hotter than Florida, the start of a season that will end sometime in late August and is best endured under a ceiling fan on a screened porch facing northeast. The Dabney High Class of '61 has rented a large conference room at the John Marshall Hotel downtown and hired a Carolinas beach music band. It is supposed to be the same band that played at their senior prom but turns out to be five other people, although some are related to the original members.

Skip rents a limousine, as a joke he claims, to pick them up at a quarter 'til 6 and later take them home. Since the driver's paid by the hour, and they don't want to arrive until 6:30 at the earliest, they have him drive them around the city while they share a bottle of champagne. They stop off at a bar near the old tobacco warehouse district for a drink, the humidity down by the river almost knocking them back in the car when they get out.

The limousine drops them off right at the John Marshall's front doors, but Nancy breaks into a sweat under her full-length teal gown during the 10 seconds they're outside, and the sweat chills her instantly when she steps into the hotel's refrigerated lobby. She realizes that she's already drunk more in one sitting than at any time since she found out she was pregnant with Wade.

The room, half of an even larger one that's been divided by a sliding panel, is large enough for 300 graduates and their spouses, should they all choose to attend. Kim Stallings has already told Nancy that no more than half have paid their $20.

Nancy doesn't see Buddy when she comes in, trailing Sandy and Skip, who provide a shield from the hugs and kisses and you-haven't-changed-a-bits while she gets her bearings.

She's adjusted to the air conditioning now and briefly considers getting a Coke at the cash bar. Then she realizes how long it might be before she has another chance to get knee-walking drunk with so little guilt. Sam's keeping Wade; she's staying at Sandy and Skip's. She orders a bourbon-and-water.

Looking around her, she sees a group of people split down the middle by the '60s, which really didn't reach Richmond and the rest of the South until the decade was almost over. The men, in particular, are a study in contrast. She sees the Dabney High quarterback, wearing a three-piece suit, his hair in a crewcut identical to the one he wore to the senior prom, talking with the all-region halfback, who is wearing a pink and purple tank top and has a handlebar moustache and hair halfway down his back. Before the night is over, they'll fight in the parking lot.

The Class of '61, Nancy thinks to herself: too young to see what Viet Nam really was, too early for integration. Those who left the old values left them after high school and didn't

seem to have much in common with their old friends anymore. She's not sure where she fits in.

There's a buffet line, and Nancy is halfway through it,
sandwiched between two men who have put on enough
weight and lost enough hair in a decade that she doesn't
recognize them, when she sees Buddy. Whether he's been
there all the time or just materialized, she doesn't know, but
there he is, 30 feet in front of her, turned to the side so
that she can see that he doesn't part his hair on the right
any more.

She picks up a couple of chicken wings and does a 180-
degree turn, not wanting to confront the past while carrying
a plate full of finger food.

But, as she sits down at the emptier end of a long table,
she feels a hand on her bare shoulder and knows it's him
before he says, "Hey, sweet potato."

She'd been his sweet potato and he'd been her sugar bear,
a long time ago. It always embarrassed him when she'd call
him that in public, but he always signed Christmas and birthday cards, "Your sugar bear."

She swallows and just looks at him as he sits down beside
her.

"You're parting your hair on the wrong side," she finally
says, and he laughs. He seems to have changed hardly at all.
He's just as handsome to her as he was the day they got
married, she realizes with a jolt. He hasn't lost the strong
Irish lines on his face to fat or age, and he still wears his
black hair straight back, the way she always liked it. Not that
many people have faces worth showing off, she used to tell
him. Don't hide your light.

Nancy has gained 10 pounds since the last time Buddy saw
her, but she feels she has hidden it well. She still has the same
ash-blond hair that they call "dirty blond" in Monacan, still
has the soft, sleepy look that was known as bedroom eyes
when she was in high school, still has a nice tan that hasn't
started to crack and dry her skin.

They ask about each other's families, talk about and to old
friends, dance around what they don't feel like talking about.
Buddy's a foreman in the pressroom now, hardly even gets
dirty any more, he tells Nancy, and they both remember the

arguments they used to have about his neglecting to wash up before he came back to their little apartment. He's bought a townhouse in the Fan and is taking management courses at Virginia Commonwealth University.

Nancy shows him the latest picture of Wade, and Buddy says he looks just like her, which she knows isn't true.

They dance the old dances, the band alternating beach music with "Go Away, Little Girl," and, late in the evening, "Moon River," which reminds them both of beach weekends at his uncle's place at Sandbridge. Nancy is struck with how a smell stays with you. She recognized Buddy right away, of course, and she knew his touch. But it's the smell, some combination of skin and hair because Buddy never did use after-shave, that really rocks her. She is all too aware that whatever senses Sam stir in her are somewhat diminished by his being second.

"I see you haven't changed your name," he says as they're dancing, and Nancy looks up in puzzlement, thinking he means her last one, but he makes a motion with his head toward Sandy and Skip dancing nearby, and she breaks up giggling, spilling her fourth bourbon-and-water on the back of Buddy's neck.

"No," she says. "I change the last one enough, so I didn't think I ought to mess with the first one. How about you? Are you still a Buddy?"

"I'm still your Buddy," he says, so low she's not sure she hears him correctly, and she lets it pass.

He says he's dating a woman, a reporter at the Times-Dispatch, but that it isn't serious. They argue a lot about politics and religion, and she wants him to have the tattoo on his arm removed.

"Tattoo?" Nancy says and breaks up again, spraying bourbon and water. "You were afraid to let them give you flu shots. Lemme see."

She finally gets him to roll up his sleeve. Sure enough, just above his right elbow the tip end of what finally reveals itself as a snake appears. The snake is a now-faded green and dominates the upper half of his right arm. He got it, he says, at a place in Wrightstown, New Jersey, while he was waiting to go to the war. It seemed right at the time, he says, and shrugs.

Nancy is transfixed. She runs her hand along the surface of the tattoo, and she feels a rush of sorrow that an arm she once loved to stroke should be mutilated so.

"Momma and Daddy blamed you," he says, and Nancy isn't sure he means for the tattoo, for his enlisting in the Army, or for their divorce. She doesn't want to ask.

Nancy and Buddy both mingle, Nancy wandering off while Buddy stays in one place and talks to whomever comes by. Nancy soon realizes that she's as predictable as one of her father's beagles on a trail, always circling back to Buddy. They'll talk for half an hour, then she'll wander off again, feeling old classmates' eyes on her.

Finally, after 1, Sandy and Skip are ready to go. Skip's called the limousine service again, and the four of them are standing there in the lobby, wobbling and laughing.

Skip invites Buddy to come over for a drink. Buddy looks at Nancy, who shrugs. They all stumble into the limousine. Skip and Sandy get in and slide over as far as they can. Buddy gets in before Nancy and, when she gets in, he slides her onto his lap. She feels warm and drowsy, and the whole experience reminds her of triple-dating in Buddy's father's Buick back in high school.

"God, I miss this," she whispers in his ear. He turns her head slightly and kisses her, and she knows that she hasn't really been kissed in years. Even during sex, Sam often doesn't kiss her, and she hadn't noticed until now that she missed the feeling. She and Buddy used to kiss and pet for what seemed like hours in her parents' den when they were sophomores in high school, welded to each other, gluttons for each other's tongues and hands, before they went on to bigger things. She realizes that Buddy seems to be a couple of degrees warmer than Sam, and she remembers what a comfort his body used to be.

"Whoah, now," Skip says. "You all going steady?"

"Fuck you, Elbert," Buddy says as he comes up for air.

The two months that Nancy and Sam have lived in Monacan have been long ones for Nancy. She's started trying to write again, using a central character loosely based on Lot, although she's still so afraid of him that she only goes to the old house when she's sure there'll be a crowd there. But she thinks he's somewhat mystical, although Sam insists that all he is, is crazy.

Sam seems happy back in his hometown, although Nancy can't help but notice that they seldom see the old friends Sam's always romanticizing about. The ones who haven't moved away don't seem to be great visitors. So, they spend a lot of time with the Chastains. They have Sunday dinner with Sam's parents, who Nancy has finally been persuaded to call Carter and Marie.

In mid-June, Sam decides that he's going to dunk a basketball. Nancy is not a big basketball fan, but she sees this as peculiar on several fronts.

First, Sam's admitted to her that he never could dunk, that even in high school, he could barely get his hand above the rim. Second, as she gently reminds him, he's 32 years old. Third, as she doesn't remind him, he's carrying about 190 pounds on his six-foot frame. Twice a year, she has to take pants to the tailor's to get new hooks put in because Sam insists he's a 34 waist.

Sam has a friend, Bobby Thacker, who works at the YMCA back in Richmond, and he's the one who put the idea in Sam's head. They were talking about high school days and basketball one Sunday afternoon back in May, watching an NBA playoff game. In the second quarter, a black player, Sam didn't even notice which one, left the floor from somewhere around the free-throw line and seemed to sail along, bringing the ball over his head with a windmill motion, then slamming it through the basket with such force that it bounced well back into the seats behind the backboard.

"God, I'd kill to be able to do that," Sam said. "I have dreams about being able to sail through the air and just slam the goddamn ball in the basket as I fly by."

"It's not impossible," Bobby told him, and he starts telling Sam about a training program that college basketball players use. Bobby can't actually dunk a basketball himself, it turns out, but he thinks he can train Sam to do it.

Bobby says he can set up a program in which Sam spends an hour on Mondays, Wednesdays and Fridays doing different kinds of hopping and jumping exercises, topped off with 10 100-yard dashes. On Tuesdays, Thursdays and Saturdays, he'll lift weights. Bobby's told him that he will have to be able to squat about twice his body weight in order to have the leg power to dunk a basketball, and Nancy's thinking that Sam had better lose a lot of weight.

Nancy thinks that her husband has forgotten all about Bobby's idea when, one Monday morning in June, she wakes up at 7 to find Sam already gone. He comes back while she's fixing breakfast, drenched with sweat. He tells her that he's decided he's going to dunk a basketball. Nancy tries to be encouraging, although she remembers that Sam did ask her the week before if she was writing another homing novel.

Nancy thinks about how Sam looks when he comes in from these morning workouts, and how he doesn't even change his workout clothes before sitting down to breakfast, a drop of sweat sometimes falling off his brow into his eggs, and she wonders if she wasn't a little too hard on Buddy's personal hygiene in their married days. Maybe, she thinks, it's just men.

Buddy helps her out of Sandy and Skip's car and into the house. She realizes she's more drunk than she's been in years, and she hopes she won't get sick. Sandy offers to make coffee, but before she can return from the kitchen with it, Buddy has taken Nancy in his arms and carried her to the guest bedroom.

Nancy's offering little resistance, but when he lays her down on the double bed, she says, "I can't do this, Buddy."

"Why can't you do this?" he asks her. "You've done it before."

"You know why. I'm afraid God will strike me dead. Or I'll be banished from Monacan."

"Sounds like a fate worse than death."

She smiles, and Buddy puts his tongue in her ear. She asks him to stop, but she knows that she won't be able to stop on her own, and she doesn't.

They make love twice that night and again in the morning, and Nancy discovers that Buddy has learned a little about pleasing since their divorce.

"I just wish we were at my place," he tells her. "I've got a basket chair that hangs from the ceiling and doesn't have a bottom . . ."

"Stop," she tells him. "They'll have to pour cold water on us."

They have breakfast with Sandy and Skip. Skip is smirking, making occasional comments that induce his wife to kick him under the table. Nancy is sure that he'll tell half the graduating class before next weekend. She's just glad that she and Sam don't socialize with the Burdens.

Buddy leaves first. Skip has to take him back to his car, which he remembers he's left in the lot at the John Marshall. Nancy and Buddy make no plans, but he gives her his phone number.

"I wish I'd known you when I was grown," he tells her.

Nancy wants to be gone before Skip gets back. She's got a hangover and is feeling a little queasy.

"You shouldn't feel bad about this," Sandy tells her. "What's a little romance between old friends? Besides, it's Sam's fault. He ought to have come with you."

Nancy answers by turning quickly and throwing up, mostly on the grass beside her car. But then she feels better, and Sandy helps her get cleaned up.

And, on the way back home, she thinks to herself, maybe it is Sam's fault.

CHAPTER ELEVEN

Nancy grew up in a family where the women did all the talking, and she's lived with Sam for more than four years, so his father's ways don't bother her.

Carter Chastain was the only one of his parents' children to go to college. He was older than most of his fellow students when he started pharmacy school in Richmond in 1920, living in a widow's boarding house and working as a janitor to help pay his way. He was always quieter than his older brothers, Lot and Warren, and the years of living by himself as a country boy in the city made him less dependent on human contact and more appreciative of silence.

He told Marie, before they were married, that he always wanted to live in Monacan, but that he was happy to be away from his home, mainly because of Lot. He told her that the happiest time of his boyhood was the two years that Lot was away in the Army. He said that Lot wrote him one time, from some camp in Texas, a rambling note full of hellfire and bile. At the end of the letter, he scribbled, "They'll be coming for you next."

He and Marie had grown up going to the same Baptist church, and he courted her in high school. She waited for him five years while he finished his schooling, then two more while he saved some money working at the drug store that Lavertis Turpin, a widower with no children, would sell to him before he died. Because Carter didn't say much, people in their community thought he would never have the nerve or spirit to ask Marie to marry him, that they'd just go on dating. But only she knew that he'd asked her to wait for him the day they graduated from high school, and she kept her vow in silence until he was ready.

Marie and Carter had a daughter, Elizabeth, who was born in 1936, in their ninth year of marriage, after they thought they couldn't have children. Three years later, their son was born, and they named him Samuel Warren Chastain, after his grandfather and his uncle, who died in France in 1918. The next year, 1940, on a day in early May, Carter came home for lunch as he usually did. The children always looked forward to his appearance, and he would play with them as much as time permitted before he went back to the store.

On this day, he did something spontaneous, which was unusual for Carter. He asked Lizzie if she would like to go with Daddy while he made some deliveries in the western part of the county. He remembered later that he'd done it because she looked so pretty in the pink, frilly dress Marie had made for her. She had her mother's dark hair and big brown eyes, and she had a disposition that made Marie the envy of every other mother in the neighborhood. Sam, who was a colicky child, was too young to go, so father and daughter took off on their big adventure.

They stopped at the drugstore first. Carter bought Lizzie a Coca-Cola while he filled the prescriptions, then he picked her up and carried her, giggling, out to the car.

He'd wanted her to sit in the back, but she wanted to be up front beside him, and he couldn't see the harm in it. Sometimes he'd let her steer the car when they went down the dirt road to his parents' house, but he told her she couldn't do that now, so she sat singing, and Carter couldn't hear "Itsy-Bitsy Spider" for the rest of his life without thinking about that day.

One second they were going down the clay road to Mrs. Haney's with her heart pills, Lizzie singing and her father day-dreaming with one arm hung out the window. The next, he was jamming the brakes instinctively as a buck deer bounded out of the woods just in time to be struck broadside by the green Chevrolet Carter and Marie had bought the year before.

The deer, hit at the peak of his leap, went over the top of the hood and into the windshield. Carter was saved by the steering wheel, but the car was disabled. All he could think to do was scoop up Lizzie's body and run toward the Haneys' house, where there might be a telephone. It was a half-mile, and Carter had to leave his burden beside the road halfway there. It took more than an hour to get an ambulance as far as Carter's broken car, from which point the two men had to walk the quarter-mile to where he'd left his daughter. Carter would always remember and never mention to anyone the bottle flies that were gathering, undisturbed, on her face and arms. They said later that she had died on impact.

Sam told Nancy that his earliest memory was being held by someone other than his mother or father in a large field, with many other people around, and of his mother taking him and saying, "You're all I've got now."

Carter has never, even for one day, forgotten how his daughter died, the sound her head made as it hit the windshield hard enough to make a perfect little starburst of a dent amid the destruction caused by the incoming deer. He refused to drive for two years after that, told old man Turpin that he'd have to either make his own deliveries or fire him and get another pharmacist.

Carter and Marie never speak to each other about Lizzie. Marie goes out on Lizzie's birthday to put flowers on her grave, which sits near the edge of the Chastain family cemetery, on a long, open hill overlooking the river. Carter goes by later the same day and again at Christmas, when he leaves a wreath and a toy. Sometimes, they're still there in July, when Marie and the other women in the family go to rid the graveyard of thorns and wisteria and empty beer cans. On those occasions, Aileen or Grace might look at the weather-beaten wreath and say, "Reckon Carter's been here," but Marie lets it pass.

Carter never had more than a two-sentence conversation with Nancy until the day she married his son, and he might not have then, she reflected, if she and her mother hadn't insisted on having at least champagne at the reception.

Carter had never really learned to dance, and Nancy had to almost drag him to the floor, then lead him around it. He'd already had two glasses of champagne, and when the music stopped, he whispered to her, "Thank you. I didn't

think I'd ever have another daughter." And he told her about
Lizzie and the emptiness she left.

"I think sometimes we might of spoiled Sam," he told her.
"We wouldn't let him do anything hardly. He had to threaten
to run away from home before I'd let him get his driver's license."

Now, though, Carter will sometimes come by in the middle
of the day to "visit" with Nancy and Wade. They'll sit on the
back porch, which has a ceiling fan. Nancy has learned to
fight the natural instinct to fill the long silences by talking
too much. If she stays quiet long enough, she's come to
understand, Carter will talk.

He tells her, over the course of a dozen visits from spring
through the middle of July, about his family and his town.
He talks about Warren, the brother who died in World War I.

"Warren was the smartest one in the family," he told her
one day, with no prelude. "If he had lived, he would of been
a lawyer or something. I was lucky I came along when I did."

He talks, with a little prompting, about how his sisters take
care of his brother Lot. Nancy knows that Carter has banned
Lot from his home because he said things about religion that
upset Marie.

"Lot thinks everybody's a hypocrite except him," he tells
Nancy on one of the rare occasions when he says anything
about his only living brother. "You stay away from him. Lot's
full of meanness."

But Nancy knows, too, that Carter goes out to Lot's trailer
sometimes, or at least he did before the vision on the barn
made it impossible to have a quiet visit.

"Carter's the one that holds things together," Grace told
her one time. "If it wasn't for Carter, I don't know what
we'd do."

Sam has inherited his father's quietness and outward de-
meanor. Nancy has seen several people at the store call him
Carter by mistake, which she finds disquieting. But Nancy
doubts that her father-in-law was ever crazy enough to make
dunking a basketball his life's ambition.

The sessions sometimes last an hour and a half now. One

73

of Sam's old classmates is the high school basketball coach, and he lets Sam have a key to the gym so that he can go early in the morning to lift weights. He's bought a weight belt, and sometimes he will make several runs at the basket, stopping just short and trying to convert horizontal speed into vertical leap. So far, he can barely touch the rim, and he can't quite lift his own weight from a squat lift.

It doesn't seem to bother Sam that everyone in town knows what he's trying to do and considers it second only to Lot's barn among the highlights of Monacan's summer entertainment. They kid him about it at church, at the drugstore, even when he and Nancy go for walks with Wade late in the evening sometimes.

Sam doesn't talk much about his quest. He does seem to be in better shape, Nancy concedes to herself.

She's seen Buddy once since the reunion in June. One Wednesday evening, she went to the largest of the Richmond malls to shop, and she saw a bank of phones, most of them taken up by teen-agers seemingly intent on keeping them for the night, but a couple on the end were empty. Before she thought about it, she'd taken the number out of her purse and called.

Buddy recognized her voice right away. She was afraid he might not be alone, but he said he was, and that he could be there in 10 minutes, but why not come to his place instead. He gave her the address, and she knew the street. Still not believing herself, she went to the car and found Buddy's townhouse, wondering what she would do if she had car trouble, or an accident, in a part of Richmond where she had no reason to be.

They made love in haste, and Buddy seemed hurt that she had to leave immediately afterward.

"When we were married, you'd rather shoot pool or drink a beer with your friends than do this," she told him while she fastened her bra.

"You don't know what you got 'til it's gone," he said, shrugging. "Like I said, I wish I'd have known you after I grew up."

She kissed him goodbye with no promises and was back in Monacan by 9:30.

Now, she's not sure. She sees the flaws in Sam through her

reacquaintance with Buddy, but she can see that Buddy hasn't achieved sainthood in the years they've been apart, either. The only time she feels guilty about any of it is when she's around Wade, who's just beginning to talk enough so that anyone can understand him.

Between his dunking program and work, Nancy doesn't have as much time with Sam as she'd like. He's more prone to fall asleep in front of the TV, and sex, which wasn't so great anyhow, now suffers by comparison.

She's still resisting working at the drugstore, and she uses the rare free moments when Wade takes a nap to write. She's not sure she'll ever like Monacan. The people, even most of the Chastains, treat her like an outsider, although they don't mind loading her down with duties. She's a part-time Sunday School teacher, an unpaid library aide and a fund-raiser for three different charities. She's expected to bake pies for the volunteer fire department's supper. When she's around other women her age from Monacan, they talk about either old times or soap operas or anybody who isn't there, and she assumes they talk about her behind her back. The word's out that she's trying to be a writer, and that seems to set her apart from her new neighbors even more. She gets into one heated (by Monacan standards) argument with a large-haired woman who's planning to sue the school board if it doesn't drop "Catcher in the Rye" from the high school book list.

"I hope you're not writing trash like that," the woman says after Nancy tells her what she thinks of book-burners.

"I wish," Nancy tells her, and then finds out later that she's the Presbyterian minister's wife. Worse yet, Sam wants her to apologize. She tells him to check the farm report.

"When it says that pigs are flying, Sweetie," she says, "you'll know I've apologized."

CHAPTER TWELVE

Had the dream about the war again, where it's 1917 and I'm shooting them big guns over there, the ones that made my ears bleed, and there's Warren, right next to me, telling me he's all right. Had it the first time a week after they told me he had died in France. Hadn't had it for, I reckon, five years.

Seems like I dream more now, usually the one about fat lightning. Maybe it's because of the barn. Maybe Jesus is trying to tell me something and I ain't smart enough to pick up on it.

I take Granger what few table scraps there is and some of that canned dog food. Reckon he's the only true friend I got. Weren't for him barking that night, I never would of knowed about the Jeter boy, never would of caught him that night, him and that girl right out there by the barn where Jesus or anybody could of seen 'em.

But I didn't run up and scare 'em or even let 'em know I seen 'em. Just slipped back in the house and bided my time. Picked up the Bible and turned it to Revelations. Sometimes you can just flip open a page or two and get a message. So I opened it, and the first thing I seen was, "Neither repented they of their murders, nor of their sorceries, nor of their fornication, nor of their thefts." I turned another page back and what my eye was pulled to, just like somebody was leading me, was, "How long, O Lord, holy and true, dost thou not judge and avenge our blood on them that dwell on the earth?"

How long, O Lord? I seen them hypocrites from the churches, all dressed up and fat and happy, eating Sunday dinner at that Morrison's I go to sometimes near-bout to Richmond. It just about makes you sick to see how pleased they all are. They can't think they'd ever do anything wrong, even though most of 'em are going around stealing from each other during the week, and they'd probably get up and walk out if a colored person was to come walking into their fine church. And the preachers would probably lead them.

It was that Reverend Boyle that Momma and Daddy took me and Holly to, not both of us together, but one at a time. It wasn't much before the Army come and got me. Holly was such a pretty little thing then, had curly blonde hair and eyes that shined like new pennies. We'd make up names for all the places around the farm, names that I told her we couldn't tell nobody else, and she swore to me that she wouldn't.

Down at the river, we'd call that Jordan. And the pond over by the property line, that was the Dead Sea.

Over on the other side of the sawdust pile, not the one now but the first one that burnt, was these weeds and little trees, and we had a cleared out spot in the middle where we could get to and nobody could find us. We called that Egypt. And Holly would come up to me when I was toting wood to the house or feeding the chickens, and she'd whisper to me, "Lot, can we go to Egypt?" I'd tell her when to meet me there. I told her above all not to tell nobody about Egypt, 'cause that was our special place. She was about the best friend I had, with Warren already working off from home and already fired up to enlist.

When Momma and Daddy took me to the preacher Boyle, first thing he said to me was, "Tell me about Egypt, Lot."

Holly went and lived off with Daddy's cousin Pete and his family. I didn't see her no more until after I had come home from the war in 1919, and even then she stayed away from me. Me and her didn't never talk about Egypt no more.

Just like Holly must of told about Egypt, the preacher must of told somebody, because they didn't nobody speak to me at church no more, and after a while, Momma called me into her and Daddy's bedroom one Sunday and said that the folks at the church was gossipers and liars, and that she didn't want me to have no more to do with 'em, that I was too good for the damn Baptists. She called them that, too. So I didn't go to church no more, but Aileen and Grace and Momma and Daddy did. That's when I quit hanging around when we had company, too. I'd go out to Egypt all by myself, or drive the car some-where.

The Army come and got me then. I know it was some of them gossipers and hypocrites in the community that told 'em where I was. Momma told 'em I'd gone down south, to North Carolina, to find work, but they come one morning and found me, in Egypt. Didn't think the fire would give me away, with all that smoke from the sawdust pile, but somebody must of told them right where to find me. Momma and Aileen and Grace and even Carter was crying when they took me off. Daddy had gone off. Some big old sergeant told me, "We got you now, boy. We goin' to feed you to the Huns. Show you what we do with chicken-shit like you." Right there where everybody could hear. And I didn't see nobody I knowed for near-bout two years.

But I didn't never forget none of it. After I come home, folks would act like I was their long-lost friend. They didn't know they kept me goin' through the war. In bayonet practice, I'd just play like it was Reverend Boyle instead of some dummy. In them trenches over in France and Germany, when sometimes we'd have to shoot 'em from 10 feet away, I'd just pretend it was some deacon or Sunday school teacher instead. Made it easy to kill people.

NOW

CHAPTER THIRTEEN

The park behind the main branch of the Richmond Public Library was meant to be a place where patrons would read "Jane Eyre" and downtown office workers would eat bag lunches and watch the seasons change. It is surrounded by grass-covered bunkers that make it look like one of the Civil War fortifications that ring the city's east side. It is shaded by Bradford pears.

On any day when the sun shines and the temperature rises above 50, though, Nancy knows she has no better than an even chance of having a bench to herself at noon. The wind-blocking bunkers and the shade the hardy trees provide were seen immediately by the city's dispossessed as a gift, and they have used it often and well.

Many of Nancy's co-workers at the library choose to eat at their desks, but she feels that if she can't have lunch outside her own building, then she's lost the whole city. The surliest wino gets a firm "no" when he asks for a handout; she only gives to those who appear to be older than herself, and she notices that they are becoming more and more scarce.

She first becomes aware of the old black woman because she is old, and because she is a woman. Most of the dispossessed are neither. While the young men hang together, she keeps mostly to herself, constantly going through a Thalhimer's shopping bag that seems almost as old as she is, rearranging what appears to be old rags and pieces of painted wood. She seems to favor red.

Sometimes, without being asked, Nancy will give a crumpled dollar to one of the few older people in the park, trying to foster the idea that she won't be forced into generosity. She tries it with the old woman one day at the end of her lunch, casually extending the gift toward the figure sitting stiffly on the bench. The old woman pushes her away, almost violently. Nancy sees for the first time that she's clutching a Bible to her chest with her left hand.

A big man in a flannel shirt and work pants, his blond hair and teeth thinning in unison, sees what happens and comes up to Nancy.

"Hey, lady, how about me? I can sure use some of that," he says, his smile twisting into a leer.

Nancy doesn't even have time to be afraid before the old woman jumps between them, her chin barely coming to the man's chest.

"Wan' me to put a spell on you?" she shouts at him. "Wan' me to? What's big old white trash like you here for? You get you a job!"

The man is taken aback. All the other homeless watch in defeated silence as he backs off.

"Anything to keep you from breathing on me, you old nigger," he says, but Nancy can see that the woman has his number somehow. She glances at Nancy and goes back to where she was sitting, alone and undisturbed.

As April dries out and becomes May, Nancy takes her lunch in the park more often, and she sees the woman every day, at the same bench, which no one else tries to take from her. She seems to have two dresses, different shades of a faded red. Her hair is steely gray and wild, never combed, and Nancy doesn't think she could weigh more than 90 pounds. She's lost most of her teeth. She occasionally appears to be drunk, but most of the time she contents herself with her Bible. She moves her lips when she reads, and sometimes she reads out loud, in a voice that is stronger than she is. It is the voice that stirs Nancy's memory first, and then she sees that the eyes haven't really changed that much.

It's been two months since Holly died, and Nancy's thoughts, for the first time in years, have willingly turned to Lot and to Old Monacan, something she'd tried to block out for 20 years. But Holly was the last, and now Nancy can look at it all again.

She drove out there, alone, went to the funeral with people she didn't know for the most part, then went by Old Monacan, or where it used to be. They left the house when they built the fancier ones around it; somebody was using it now for an antique shop. She saw right away that the barn was gone. The best she could tell, it was underneath the deck of a three-story Colonial home that backed up to the old Chastain place. She wondered if the people who owned the house knew what they'd built over. She deduced that the sawdust pile was somewhere under what was now the foundation of a sprawling contemporary.

She felt a stab of pain, walking through the weeds in front of the old house. She reached down to pick a jagged piece of wood out of her pantyhose, just above the ankle. It was, she saw when she held it up, fat lightning, so oily she thought she could feel its substance ooze through the pine wood. She threw it down and left.

But ever since that February day, she's been thinking about it, and a part of her already knows that she's going to write about it, now that nobody is left to be embarrassed.

And now, she thinks, this.

One warm day, a day that made her think of the one 20 years before, when she and Sam left Richmond for Monacan, she has an idea. She goes to her closet and finds a dress that she can stand to part with, a dress of cardinal red with a black belt. She puts it in a plastic bag and carries it to work.

At lunch, she brings her yogurt and apple to the park, along with the plastic bag. She thinks at first that the old lady isn't there, that she's moved on after all these weeks. But then there's a rustle in the bushes and the woman comes into view, moving stiffly. She dismisses with a wave of her arm a black man who looks to be half her age. He looks back resentfully, but he moves on.

Nancy finishes her lunch, then walks over and hands the bag to the old woman. She starts to push it away, but something catches her eye. The red.

She snatches it away from Nancy and lets the bag fall to the ground as she holds up a red dress to outshine her other two.

"Wook!" she exclaims, and the park's other residents whistle and shout.

The old woman looks back at Nancy, holds out her right hand, the one with the bracelet, and Nancy shakes it, turning it slightly so that she can read the name that encircles her wrist.

"Sebara," Nancy says.

"Lot's nephew's wife," Sebara says, and Nancy knows that the woman has known it was her all along.

It's then that Nancy knows she's ready to write.

1971

CHAPTER FOURTEEN

By late July, the crowds of pilgrims coming to see Jesus on the barn have grown to the point that the county sends a full-time deputy sheriff out every evening an hour before sunset to direct traffic. Now, due to some irregularity on the barn's surface or the shadow of a tree branch, there appears to be a line running from the figure's right eye to the bottom of its face.

Lot sees what it is as soon as the people first notice it.

"It's tears," he says. "It's Jesus shedding his tears for this here sinful world." And somebody mutters "Amen" in the back of the crowd.

With every new trick of the light, some new aspect is seen or imagined by the people, many of whom have driven hundreds of miles out of their way on vacation to see the vision. Dozens of people a day pull in at the stores in Monacan itself to ask directions to Lot's home, because the only dateline in the news stories they've seen is "Monacan, Va." To reduce confusion, a sign is placed at the entrance to the county road to Old Monacan. It reads: Jesus-on-the-barn. An arrow points the way.

Simon Jeter complains to the sheriff's department that his crops are being ruined by all the people parking on the edge of his fields. One afternoon in June, he leaves his Buick in the garage and moves his oldest son's Ford pickup beside the garage, blocking the way to Lot's. Cars are backed up almost to the state highway before the deputy sheriff comes and threatens to give Jeter a citation for obstructing traffic.

But Jeter doesn't have much time to devote to keeping Lot's pilgrims off his property. His second-oldest son's boy, Terry, is still missing. They first assumed that the boy had run away again, and they checked with all their relatives and acquaintances where they thought he might have gone. But the boy doesn't show up.

Now, a month later, they have his picture on posters in stores throughout the northern half of the county. They even put one beside the dirt road leading past Jeter's to Lot's, hoping one of the pilgrims will have seen Terry somewhere. But no one admits to having seen the boy.

"It's one of them damned foreigners that Lot Chastain's got out at his place," Jeter tells Sheriff Watson. "Ain't no telling where-all them people are coming from. Some of 'em looks like gypsies to me. They liable to do anything."

The sheriff tells Jeter that it isn't likely that somebody could have kidnapped Terry at the Chastain place because there's always a crowd there, but he promises to have his deputy keep an eye on the pilgrims.

"If I was you-all, I wouldn't worry all that much," the sheriff tells the Jeters. "He's run off before, and I expect he'll run off again. He'll turn up."

"Ain't never been gone a month before," the boy's father says in a low voice.

"Well," the sheriff says, scratching his head, "he's gettin' older."

Nancy is still coming out once a week, most recently with Aileen and Grace. There's been an offer on the farm, one that would allow Lot to keep the house, the land around it and the road leading in. The buyer is offering $450,000 for the rest of the land, taking up most of what was once the town of Old Monacan. He plans to build an upscale housing development, with a new road coming in back of Jeter's property.

Because Lot's mother didn't leave a will, no one knows what to do about the family estate. Lot, Carter and their sisters divvied up the 100-acre plot their father owned and farmed across the river, and all of them except Lot sold their 20-acre parcels. They all believe Lot when he tells them that his mother, right before she died, said the house and the land around it were his as long as he lived. However, none of them are willing to turn down that much money for land that isn't even being farmed.

"Honey," Aileen says to Nancy as she explains the situation, "I wouldn't mind it if I didn't have to sit on a footstool for the rest of my life, trying to sell shoes to white trash that don't change their socks every day. I wouldn't mind retiring."

"I just don't know what gets into him," Grace says. "He used to could be so nice sometimes."

"When?" Aileen snaps.

"Well," Grace says, "he used to buy us candy at the store sometimes, when we were young'uns."

"Yeah," Aileen says, "and then he'd make us sing a song before he'd give it to us, and sometimes he'd make us sing, and then he wouldn't give it to us anyhow."

"Now, I don't remember that," Grace says. "And besides, he's our brother."

"And he does need a keeper," Aileen says.

"Well, I just hope he doesn't have one of his spells. Let's try to not get him excited."

They come on a Wednesday. It takes them 45 minutes to get from the state highway to the house, and they see that there are perhaps 200 people there. They have to go around a bus that has "Ebenezer Free Will Gospel Holiness Church" across the side of it. The bus is painted purple, and there's a picture of a black Jesus on the back of it.

"Even the niggers are coming now," Aileen says.

Most nights, the crowd is either all white or close to it. There isn't one white church in Moseby County that has a black member, and there isn't a black church that has one white member. Even in the area of miracles, crowds run along racial lines.

But tonight, it appears that the entire Wednesday night congregation of the Ebenezer Free Will Gospel Holiness Church has decided to take a field trip. About 60 black people stand, all together and to one side, and wait for Jesus-on-the-barn to appear. One woman, with curly reddish hair that shines in the late-afternoon light, seems to be their leader. She is wearing a scarlet robe, and everyone gives her room.

Lot stands back from the crowd, as is his custom, and Aileen, Grace and Nancy go and stand beside him. Lot nods. Billy Basset, who's become a fixture around the barn and helps Lot with chores, stands a little to one side.

The magic moment comes. Most of those present haven't seen it before, and a murmur slowly rises. Sometimes, Lot feels obligated to go forward and point out an arm here, a foot there, a crown of thorns up there, but this crowd picks up the general outline more quickly than most.

The Chastains become aware of a rising, rhythmic chant over to one side, and they see that the focus is shifting between the barn itself and the black woman in the scarlet robe.

Finally, they can hear her repeating, and her followers repeating with her: "GLOOORRY to God on high, GLOOORRY to his only son," over and over. It isn't quite singing, but it reminds Nancy of the old blues records that Buddy used to like to listen to. Soon, even some of the white people are at least mouthing the words. The chant goes on until the last vestiges of the image have faded from the side of the barn.

While the crowd is breaking up, the woman in scarlet goes straight to Lot, who is acknowledging thanks from pilgrims as they go past and occasionally offering them a terse bit of Revelation.

"Praise Jesus," she says, by way of greeting. "Brother Lot, I am Sister Sebara Tatum of the Ebenezer Free Will Gospel Holiness Church. We are awed by your vision."

Lot just nods. She reaches inside her robe and produces a business card that has her name, her church's name and address, a cross and the words: "God is All." And then she is gone.

"Well, I reckon they'll all be coming out here now," Aileen says with a sigh.

"Who do you mean, 'they'?" Lot asks, turning to her.

She sees the warning signs and tries to avert trouble.

"Oh, you know what I mean, Lot. Everybody."

"Naw," he says. "You don't mean everybody. You mean black folks. Reckon you think Jesus is too good for them. Reckon Jesus ought to be segregated, like that fine brick church you all go to. I suppose you'd call in the National

Guard if them folks tried to go to your church one fine Sunday morning."

"Now, Lot," Grace starts, "Aileen didn't mean nothing."

Billy Basset has slipped away to his tent down toward the river, where he'll stay until he's sure Lot is in for the night. People in the crowd sense trouble and either stop to stare or move a little more hurriedly to their cars and vans. Nancy sees that Lot's face is almost as red as the black woman's dress, and that his eyes seem to be all black. A little boy wanders away from his parents and bumps into Lot. He looks up into Lot's face and runs screaming toward his father.

"Come on, Lot," Aileen says. "Let's go over to your place and talk."

They finally get him away from the departing crowd and into the trailer, where the living room is too hot and too small for four people, but they can't get him to change the subject. Aileen broaches the subject of the offer on the land, but Lot doesn't even want to listen. He goes into a 15-minute diatribe against churches in general and Monacan Baptist in particular. Finally, Aileen has had enough.

"I don't have to put up with this shit," she says as Grace tries to shush her and Nancy makes her first move toward the only door. "I came out here because somebody wants to make all of us rich. Somebody wants to let you keep Momma and Daddy's house and the yard and the road and still give us near-bout half a million dollars. I . . . ."

She stops talking. She's almost as red as Lot is now, and she starts crying. "Oh, Lot, why can't you act right?"

"You all are just trying to sell the place out from under me," he says. "You must think I'm an idiot. This here land won't never be sold, not as long as I live."

He turns then to Nancy, who hasn't said anything except "hello" so far.

"And I reckon you've been sending this girl out here to soften me up," he says, as Nancy wrestles with the doorknob. "Get me so you can make me do whatever you want. Well, it ain't a-gonna work."

Nancy finally gets the door open, just before Lot gets there. She stands outside, not knowing which way to run, for five

minutes. Finally, Aileen and Grace come out, in no particular
hurry. There's no sign of Lot.

In the car, Nancy starts to ask what happened after she
left.

"Lot just gets overexcited," Grace says.

"He's just full of meanness," Aileen adds. Then she sighs.
"I reckon I might as well plan on selling a few thousand
more pairs of shoes."

Sam continues to do his plyometric exercises, running and
jumping one day, lifting the next. He's gaining about an inch
a month, but something happens in late July that sets him
back.

He's in the gym between 7 and 7:30 one morning, lifting
weights in the locker room, when he hears the door open,
and two black kids, members of the high school basketball
team, come walking in. The coach has also given them a key
so they can work out with weights before school, but they're
obviously more intent on playing basketball. They become
quiet when they see Sam, dress quickly and take a couple of
basketballs out on the court with them.

Sam finishes his squats. He's lost about five pounds and
can now lift his weight, straining to keep his knees from
buckling as he dips and then rises with his arms gripping
the bar as it digs into his shoulders and the back of his neck.
He does five repetitions, does some more leg lifts, then gets
ready to go home and shower.

He's feeling pretty good about himself when he decides to
peek in on the two basketball players. He opens the door to
the gym halfway, his weight belt in his hand. The two teen-
agers aren't really playing; they're setting each other up.

One throws the ball up on the backboard from about five
feet away. The other, who has already started running from
the top of the key, jumps as he nears at the basket, just as
the ball is coming off the glass. The point is to catch the ball
in midair, preferably with one hand, and dunk it as spectacu-
larly as possible. About half the time, the coordination is just
off. The other half, Sam is struck by how the players seem
to have another gear, seem to actually rise to another level
after they've apparently reached the peak. Their hands seem

to be a good foot and a half over the rim at the top of their leaps. Sam realizes that probably neither of them has ever lifted a weight in his life unless a coach was standing right behind him. He resists an urge to throw the $30 weight belt in the trash can by the door.

Sam and Nancy are having Sunday dinner with his parents when they hear about the body. Holly and her husband, Cole, are also there, sitting around the big drop-leaf maple table in the Chastains' dining room. Marie answers the phone, and she has the quiet, flushed look of a bearer of news when she comes back.

"They think they've found that boy's body," she says as she sits down.

"Who? The Jeter boy?" Carter asks her.

She gives him a look that silently asks how many boys have turned up missing in Monacan lately, then says, "Yes. Down by the river. A dog dragged up a human skull and part of a spine, Sue Wampler said. Dragged it right up in Wilbur Mangum's yard, that used to work at the court house. Berlean was the one that found it, and they had to take her to the hospital with chest pains. Sue said Johnny was there, with the rescue squad, and they're looking for more now."

"They think there's more than one?" Cole asks.

"More, uh, body parts," Marie says.

Everyone looks down at their roast beef.

"Johnny says they might even be searching down on the back side of Momma and Daddy Chastain's land," Marie goes on.

"The Mangums live right back of where Daddy dug the irrigation pond," Carter says. "I think he sold them that land."

Holly, without looking up from dinner, says, "The Dead Sea."

"The what?" her husband asks as Carter clears his throat.

"Oh," she turns her head, obviously embarrassed, "that's just what Lot used to call that pond. The Dead Sea."

She looks up and around the table. "But don't tell him I told you that."

Nancy wants to ask her why not, but Sam gently presses his right arm against her left, and she remains quiet.

Nancy hasn't seen Buddy since the night she called him from the mall. She's writing again, and she's hoping that the lack of opportunity will conspire to keep them out of the same bed. She finds it odd that, after living in the same city as her ex-husband for six years, she had to move 30 miles away to rediscover him.

But, the Thursday night after Terry Jeter's body was found, she's in Richmond again, having dinner with her parents. Sam, as usual, is too tired to make the trip with her, so she and Wade go alone.

She finds that she misses Suzanne and Pat, the former for her vivaciousness, the latter for the quiet sense of steadiness he always seemed to lend to their home. She visits them as much now as when she lived in Richmond, and with less of a feeling of obligation. Sam's silence often strikes her as moodiness, and on those occasions she wonders if she's offended him without realizing it. Now, with Buddy back in the world, she is aware that every unexplained gap in the conversation has her steeling herself for accusations.

Thinking of her father and of Carter, she wonders if it just takes men longer to grow up.

"Honey," Suzanne tells her when she verbalizes this theory, "I don't think they ever do."

Candy's still living at home, saving money to buy a condominium, and she's watching TV and helping Nancy catch up on Richmond gossip. Robbie comes in while they're there; he's still living at home, too, with another year of college left. Marilou calls to talk to her mother.

Nancy remembers her house as always being like this. Her father complained that he was going to move to the bus station so he'd have more privacy, but he knew the name of every neighborhood kid, and they all seemed to be drawn to him. His quietness made them all the more appreciative when he would show them a trick or play catch with them. And Suzanne, who looks the same to Nancy now as she did 20 years ago, always had something going. She'd have neighborhood pet shows, managing to give every toad and hamster some kind of prize. Nancy wonders if she and Sam will ever have the kind of house where something's always happening.

On the way home, with Wade already asleep in the car seat in the back, Nancy stops and calls Buddy. This time, she tells him, she really can't come over, because of the child. OK, he says, where are you? Finally, she tells him, and he's there, in a mini-mall parking lot, in 15 minutes.

Buddy slides into the passenger seat, and Nancy looks nervously into the back, where Wade's head is slumped to the right at a 45-degree angle and his mouth is hanging open in blissful unconsciousness.

"Don't worry," he says. "They can sleep through anything."

"How would you know?" she asks him.

He responds by putting his left arm around her neck and drawing her to him. They kiss.

"I can't do this," Nancy says. "Not with Wade in the back seat."

They talk softly for a few minutes, then Buddy starts sliding his hand up her thigh so casually that she doesn't resist at first.

"Just like high school," he says, reaching around her shoulder to fondle her left breast, finding her nipple beneath her blouse and bra and giving it a squeeze with his thumb and forefinger.

"Yeah. Tenth grade," Nancy whispers, unzipping Buddy's pants while he helps her slide down her pantyhose.

"Third base," Buddy says, continuing to stroke her as she reciprocates.

Then Nancy becomes aware of Buddy pushing her head downward with his free hand.

"I think we just graduated," she says before sinking below the dashboard.

Putting her panties and pantyhose back on, Nancy is amazed to realize that they've only been together for 15 minutes.

"We're going backwards," he says. "Every time I see you, I see you less."

"Buddy," she says, trying to soothe him, but she hears an echo from the back seat.

"Buddy." Wade is wide awake, as if he's never been asleep. He's grinning a two-year-old's grin. "Buddy."

Buddy doesn't know whether to jolly the child or run. He hurriedly zips up his pants while Nancy adjusts her skirt and worries about the stain on her blouse.

"Go back to sleep, sweetie," she says. "You're just having a dream." She doesn't even acknowledge Buddy as he quietly exits from the passenger side.

CHAPTER FIFTEEN

The state medical examiner confirms that the human skull and upper spine dragged up by Wilbur Mangum's dog are part of the late Terry Jeter, and that he evidently drowned in the irrigation pond near the back of the Chastain property, down by the river. The examiner's office says his skull could have been crushed when it struck one of the stumps beneath the surface. The body apparently was caught in some of the underwater vegetation that almost completely clogs the pond, and when it somehow dislodged and surfaced, it was found, dragged to shore and torn apart by the neighborhood dogs. It is Simon Jeter who tells the sheriff that his grandson couldn't swim.

Two days later, Lot disappears.

Carter comes by to talk with him about the developer's offer on their land and finds only Granger and Billy Basset. The boy has unchained Lot's dog and is sitting with him in the shade of a sycamore tree in the mid-afternoon heat. Billy says that Lot was gone when he came to the house that morning, and that he let himself into the trailer and fed Granger. Lot's been known to drive off and not be seen for several days, so Carter normally wouldn't be worried, but the Jeter boy's death has him spooked. He's also worried that, despite all the "Posted" signs Lot has put around the property, Terry Jeter's family will try to blame the Chastains for the boy's drowning.

"Mr. Chastain," Billy asks Carter, "what'll I do about all the pilgrims?"

Carter gives him a puzzled look.

"You know. The pilgrims that come to look at Jesus on the barn. What'll I tell them?"

97

"Don't reckon you'll have to tell 'em anything," Carter says. "You might stick around, though, to make sure they don't start taking pieces off of it for holy relics."

Then Carter tells Billy not to worry, that Lot's disappeared before, but that he always turns up.

"You ought to look out around here, though," he says. "Don't your folks mind you being out here after what happened to that Jeter boy?"

"They don't care," Billy says.

"Well, you be careful."

Carter backs away from Billy and Granger; the dog once chased him up the same sycamore tree.

Billy's worries about the pilgrims are solved, for one day at least, when a low-pressure system brings in a thunderstorm by 4 o'clock and more clouds and a steady, drenching rain, first messenger of autumn, behind it. A few out-of-towners drive down the old road in the rain just to see the barn, but there'll be no visions of Jesus today.

The sheriff has already been around to talk to Billy and to Lot. Billy hadn't seen Terry or known anyone who had seen him for a month before his body was dragged up in pieces. He'd just assumed that Terry had decided to run away again; he'd tried to talk Billy into hitch-hiking to California with him back in late May, said he had cousins in some place called Bakersfield.

It does make Billy feel a little uneasy to think about Terry drowning. Both boys had played around the pond, but the vegetation in it had long since choked out the fish, and the river was within eyesight anyhow, for anyone who wanted to fish or swim. Billy knew Terry couldn't swim, without really having to be told. When the water would get low enough to wade to French Crossing, he never could get Terry to come across with him, and he noticed that Terry never got very far from the bank when they'd go skinny-dipping in the river.

He must have got careless, is Billy's final judgment on his late acquaintance.

Billy is proud of not getting careless. He's made enough money selling off the Chastains' smaller valuables, the ones tucked away inside plunder rooms and cubbyholes, to keep himself going. He will spend a few days once in a while across the river with his mother and grandmother and the usual revolving door of relatives and boyfriends, and he's bought and sold some dope, just about breaking even, but he always returns to Lot's, where he can camp by the river until Lot's light goes out and then slip into the house to sleep or plunder, according to his mood. His fence tells him that, soon, he'll send him to Florida in a new car that somebody else will load down there. The police will never find the stuff, and all Billy will have to do to make $300 is drive it back. Billy's never been out of Virginia, and he wonders if Florida is as far away as California. But at least he won't have to hitchhike.

Nancy hasn't been out to the Chastain place since her run-in with Lot the night they met Sebara Tatum. She spends most of her time either writing or taking care of Wade and Sam. Sam hasn't asked her to help out at the drugstore lately, for which she's grateful.

She takes Wade for a walk every day. They go down Maple, stopping to let whatever housewives or retired couples might be outside make a fuss over the boy. Nancy is concerned that Wade might not have too many friends his age if they stay in Monacan, because everyone of child-bearing age seems to have left. The best she can figure, there aren't five children under the age of six among the town's 600 or so residents.

When she asks Sam about this, he tells her that there are lots of young families out of town, out in the county. The children she's seen, though, standing dirty and open-mouthed beside cinder-block houses and mobile homes on the way in and out of town, she can't imagine as companions for her son. She feels like a snob, and she keeps her opinions on the matter to herself.

Nancy and Wade go along the sidewalks that line each of the six side streets feeding into Mosby Street, the east-west spine that leads to the town's head, Courthouse Square. The walk to the courthouse, with stops to visit and for Wade to squat along the concrete walk and inspect a line of ants or an acorn, takes 20 minutes. It might have seemed tedious to Nancy two years before, but now she finds that, on rainy days, she misses the slow daily meander. The town is so small that there is no place in it where a person can stand and, in taking a 360-degree turn, not see its edges. Even at Courthouse Square, the stalks of a corn field are visible just beyond the Chieftan Diner.

Nancy and Wade often go inside the Monacan Drug Store to say hello to Sam, who is sometimes too busy to talk. If Nancy sees that he's waiting on a customer, she'll just wave and tell Wade that Daddy's working, which displeases the boy considerably.

Courthouse Square is across the street from most of Monacan's stores. Its neoclassic center was meant for the larger town that local leaders expected in the future, but Monacan didn't grow, and most of the town's business can still be conducted in the original courthouse building. A small jail, seldom used, is connected by a walkway. There is a historical marker out front, and the large expanse of grass between the courthouse itself and the streets bordering it are the closest thing to a park that Monacan has. Here, Nancy sits on a shady bench while Wade chases squirrels. By the time they've walked back to their rented house on Maple, it's time for Wade's nap and for Nancy to write for an hour before starting dinner.

Lately, Wade has learned a new word. At unexpected moments, whenever he sees a man with sandy-brown hair of a certain size and look go by, he'll cry out "Buddy!" Sometimes the man will turn and smile at Nancy and the child, or merely look puzzled. Wade does this several times when Sam's with them, and Nancy is sure her husband can feel her cringe.

"Am I your buddy?" he asks Wade once, but the boy just points at a departing figure and says, again, "Buddy!" When Sam's not along, Nancy tells Wade "No" every time he says the name, but the boy is well into his Terrible Twos, and this only encourages him.

The second night that Lot is missing, it's still raining. Aileen persuades Grace to come with her to the old family home so they can see if their brother has returned yet. The two women slosh through mud puddles in Aileen's Buick and Grace wonders aloud what will happen if they get stuck.

"Hush, Grace," Aileen says as the car's right side sinks down almost to the axle in a hole made deeper by all the traffic of late. "If we get stuck, we'll just go back to Simon Jeter's and get some help."

They come around the last bend, Aileen's headlights striking one of the few remaining chimneys in Old Monacan. The leaning pile of bricks shines brightly in the sudden light, causing Grace to let out a little squeal that scares Aileen as much as the sight of the chimney, which she doesn't remember her headlights ever hitting just that way before. She thinks to herself that Grace's nerves are getting worse.

Lot's trailer is dark, and Aileen stops beside it, the Buick's engine idling while she debates whether to go in. It's after 9; if Lot were back, he'd still be up, with the lights on. Besides, his car's missing.

"Look, Aileen," Grace says, leaning low to see something higher than the car's windshield. Aileen looks, and finally sees what Grace is pointing toward. In the back of their parents' old house, there's a light, just barely visible through the mist. They watch it for a few seconds, then it suddenly disappears.

"I wonder if we oughtn't to call the police," Grace says, and Aileen doesn't say anything.

"No," she says finally. "It might have been just the way the headlights were hitting the house. Or something." She's not sure herself, and she turns the car around in the little grass patch in front of Lot's trailer instead of driving up to the open area in front of the old house, trying not to spook Grace any more while she's doing it.

"I wish Lot'd let us sell this place," Grace says when they're back on the paved road headed out.

"Hush, Grace," Aileen says, but she's thinking the same thing.

Upstairs, Billy sits in the dark, the darkened flashlight in his hand, and looks out the window at the headlights down below. He's taking advantage of Lot's absence to give the old house a more thorough going-over than he's done before, but all he's been able to find are some silver dollars in the back of an old chest-of-drawers.

He breathes a sigh of relief when the car turns around, but he knows he'd better spend the rest of this night in his tent by the river, no matter how much it rains. It crosses his mind that he might have to accept the fact that he's gotten about all he's going to out of the old house. He would leave— the old man certainly isn't much fun to be around; you never can tell when he's going to launch into a tirade about something Billy's never even noticed. But the image on the barn, and all the people who come every day the weather's willing, treating Lot and even Billy like they're special, somehow makes him think it will be worth his while to stay, at least until it turns cold.

In late August, during the week that Lot disappears, Sam and Nancy go to visit Sam's second cousin, Pete Bondurant, who wants to give them some of his surplus of garden vegetables. Pete lives off Route 17, between the water tower and the river, right behind the Riverview Drive-In, the only drive-in theater in the county. Even though they know they'll be keeping him up past his bedtime, they take Wade along, too, because Pete and his wife, May, haven't seen him since Christmas.

The Riverview Drive-In has shown general-interest films for most of its life, but nobody wants to sit outside and watch movies without air conditioning or heat any more, buying a Pic and lighting the spiral contraption to fend off mosquitoes. So, a year ago, the owners went to the only thing that still attracted customers to drive-in movies in the '70s—X-rated. Since she first got a look at what X-rated meant, May Bondurant, with Pete offering moral support, has tried to get the county to at least make the Riverview build a higher fence.

When Sam and Nancy turn off Route 17 onto the rut road leading to Pete's house, a quarter-mile away, it's still twilight, and the rain has finally stopped. They can see the blank screen to their left, another quarter-mile from the Bondurants' back porch, and hear the bass notes from whatever music is piped in before the show starts.

"Daddy said that Pete cut down a perfectly good chinaberry tree the month after they started showing skin flicks," Sam says. "Gave him a perfect view of the screen."

Pete Bondurant, a heavy-set, bald man with deep smile wrinkles, looks vaguely like the Chastains. He has brought

102

two watermelons out of the patch, and May has two Winn-Dixie bags full of field peas and another one of tomatoes. Sam and Nancy sit with them on the porch for a while, talking and drinking iced tea. Nancy is seated facing Pete, holding Wade in her lap, with nothing but fields between her and the Riverview's screen.

When the coming attractions start, swatches of indecipherable music and an occasional low moan can be heard over the porch fan. Despite their repeated complaints, Pete and May have become so inured to the Riverview's fare that they don't even mention it. Nancy is glad that it's dark, so that no one can see her blush. She gets distracted and has to ask May to repeat something twice, and she's glad when they can finally leave.

Wade's asleep by the time they've rounded the circular drive and are headed back to the highway. Halfway to the road, Sam slows down and looks to his right, across the beanfields to where a young blonde woman is having sex with two black men at the same time.

"Ever been to one of those?" he asks Nancy.

"No. . . . Well, yeah, a bunch of us one time all went to the Lee X in Richmond. But that was indoors. . . . and I think all they showed was tits."

At the road, Sam turns right instead of left, then takes the dirt road that leads to the Riverview's entrance.

"What about Wade?" Nancy asks, but Sam assures her that he'll sleep through anything. She doesn't dispute him. A girl too young to be legally admitted to the Riverview's double-features takes their money, glancing at the sleeping child in the back seat.

They park two-thirds of the way back, behind the brick hut that houses the projection room, snack bar and restrooms. The Riverview still has the heavy, head-shaped metal speakers, and Sam manages to hook the one nearest to the car window after dropping it to the ground once.

He slides over from behind the steering wheel as they start watching a feature that's already begun, about a housewife who's seduced by a young stranger and then blackmailed into committing various sexual gymnastics with other strangers, supposedly against her will.

"That what you do when I'm out working?" he asks Nancy as he slides his hand up her thigh. She turns a little, kissing him as he strokes her through her jeans.

"Yeah," she says. "Two or three at a time sometimes," and she feels him growing in her hand. "I just can't help myself. What about you and that clerk? Do you two take some long, hard breaks in the afternoon? Hmmm?"

Sam whispers things in her ear that she's never heard him say before, but she realizes that they're about to engage in sex for the first time in about a month, and she's willing to go along. She can remember when Sam wanted to make love to her all the time, and she never knew she'd miss those times so much, so soon.

The front seat is too crowded, with Sam, Nancy and the steering wheel. She sheds her jeans and panties and straddles him. Sam is able to wedge himself between the seat and the wheel, and Nancy rides him, realizing that they're fogging up the windows like a couple of teen-agers.

Afterward, as Nancy struggles to get dressed, Sam tries to rise and accidentally rests his left hand on the steering wheel's horn button. The loud blare is answered by two or three other cars in the general vicinity, and all the noise wakes up Wade.

Sam raises his head up and looks into the back seat, where their son seems to be wide awake.

"Buddy!" the boy exclaims.

CHAPTER SIXTEEN

That Wednesday night, I wasn't expecting nothing. It was the heat that done it, I reckon.

After what that Basset boy calls the pilgrims had left, and he'd gone on back to his tent by the river, it was still too hot, and I got me a sudden urge to go riding with the window down. The air-conditioner in my trailer don't work so good, and besides, nothing feels good as that cool night air whipping by at 55 miles an hour.

So I fed Granger and then got the keys to the truck and took off, headed out to Route 17 and then up towards the river, nowhere special in mind. Crossed over, feeling that cool wind whipping up my shirt sleeve and something made me turn left, towards Murro.

Now, I hadn't been to Murro in years. No reason to. Ain't nothing there but a few colored folks that can't afford to leave. Before the war, me and Warren used to come up here to the bootleggers. But Warren didn't like to take me drinking with him.

What took me to Murro, I don't know, but soon as I passed the old town sign nobody'd bothered to take down, I seen the other one: Ebenezer Free Will Gospel Holiness Church, and I didn't know right off where I seen the name before. Then it come to me. Right there in my billfold. On that card she give me.

I hadn't never been in no colored church before. Just ain't done. But something told me to turn in. It wasn't nothing but a old white frame church that looked like it needed a paint job. Probably used to be the white church and then it wasn't good enough for 'em, so they let the coloreds have it. Just don't let 'em try to go to the white church. Damn hypocrites.

There was a covered place outside with benches, where they have picnic on the grounds, I reckon, and old rotten wood steps leading up to the porch. A couple of colored men my age, might of been deacons, just looked at me when I went in, and one started towards me and stopped, but they didn't say nothing.

Something led me in there, and I took a seat in the back, took my hat off. I could see right off there wasn't another white person in there, but after some of them stared at me, they seemed like they forgot I was there.

I couldn't hardly blame 'em. It was a service to make you forget. Wasn't like them mealy-mouthed sermons the Baptists used to have. And the one giving it to 'em was Sebara Tatum.

It wasn't like she was talking. Even before I got inside, I could hear the low moans and the organ music. Inside, it was sweaty and smelled like collard greens, and Sebara was giving 'em hell.

She was wearing that same blood-red robe she had on when they'd come to the barn to see Jesus, and her hair looked like it was copper in the light of that old church. She was light-skinned and didn't have one of them big flat noses like some of 'em has. She was right pretty. Sebara Tatum'd say a few words between breaths, a-saying some and a-singing some, with the organist hitting a note while she took another breath and them colored folks in the pews going, "Uh-huh," and "Tell it, sister Sebara" and I don't know what-all else.

She'd lift her arms up towards heaven and say, "And the LOOOORRD told Adam," singing the "Lord" part. Then she'd take a breath, then go, "He said GOOOO and be fruitful," another breath, then, "But old SLEEEWWWFOOOT Satan," another breath, then, "He SAAAIID to Eve," another breath, "you can BEEE like God," and she went on like that for must of been 45 minutes, some people crying and falling in the aisles. One woman got so caught up in the spirit that she throwed her baby right down in the aisle, and the young'un just looked up at her. Didn't even cry.

And Lord it was hot. Must of been 100 degrees in there. But something made me stay right through it all.

And then, right at the end, she seen me back there at the back.

She pointed right at me, all them colored folks' red eyes turning my way, and said, "We HAAVE in our midst . . . one that has SEEEEN the sign . . . of the ALMIGHTY Lord . . . He has been VISITED by the Lord . . . A SIGN has come to him . . . He has been BLESSED with the image . . . of our LORD Jesus Christ . . . right there on the SIIIDE . . . of a HUMBLE barn . . . Jesus has TOUCHED him . . . BLESSED are you."

And the colored folks are nodding and saying, "Blessed are you," too, and then they break out into a song I ain't heard in church before, and people are dancing and praising Jesus, and that goes on for 20 minutes, me clapping and singing along with the rest of 'em, and I'm wondering what these folks do on Sundays.

Sebara Tatum comes right for me when it's over, waiting for some of the colored ladies to thank me for coming, me not knowing what to say. Then she tells me, "Follow me." And I do.

She leads me over across the church yard to where she's got this here Lincoln automobile, and she tells me to get in it. We get in, colored people staring a hole in us from the church yard.

"I prayed you'd come," she says, and then she starts up the car, and we go back to her place. She lived in this cinder-block house, right by the highway, couldn't hardly get that Lincoln in between the road and house. Looked like it used to be a store.

She went to the door and unlocked it and then looked at me like she was wonderin' what I was waiting for. I got out.

"We're going to be a team, Mr. Chastain," she said. "We're going to build a shrine for Jesus." And then she did something nobody'd done for a long time. She kissed me. Right on the lips.

People think old folks is supposed to not think about all that stuff any more, but sometimes I just can't help it. Sebara kept me there all night, told me such stuff that would make any old man feel right good. She didn't want to turn the light off, but I ain't too keen on some woman seeing all of me.

Afterwards, I had that dream again, where I'm eating fat lightning. Only this time, it's Sebara that's serving it up to me, in a bowl, and she laughs and laughs when I start to eating it.

We stayed there for two days and nights more, eating tomato sandwiches and Chef-Boy-Ar-Dee spaghetti out of cans, and then Sebara told me, on the morning of the third day, "Rise up, Lot Chastain. We got work to do."

And she made me get dressed, took me back to the church to get my truck, and we both drove on back to Old Monacan.

People say I ain't got good sense, but Sebara is just like Momma used to be. She told me, "It ain't you that's crazy, Lot. It's them. You seen the savior. They too dumb to."

I reckon it was God's will that took me to Murro that night.

CHAPTER SEVENTEEN

On Saturday afternoon, Aileen comes by. The cool weather in the wake of the storm is drifting back into summer, but the sky's still bright blue and the window air conditioner is still silenced. Sam is napping on the chaise lounge on the back porch and Wade's asleep in his crib. Nancy's writing in the study, so she's the one who hears the door bell.

Aileen looks distracted. She walks inside without speaking and looks around, then lowers her voice as if she's afraid someone will hear.

"Lot's come back," she tells Nancy, "and he's brought a colored woman with him."

Sam comes in, rubbing his eyes, and Aileen tells them both the whole story, or what she knows of it.

"Did you tell Daddy already?" Sam asks her.

"I told him. He acted like it wasn't none of my business, or none of his. Said Lot was bound to do something crazy; it was just a matter of what is it this time."

Aileen persuades Sam to drive her up to Old Monacan, and Nancy decides she'll go, too. She gets Wade up and dresses him. By the time they get to Lot's, it's past 4 o'clock, too early for the pilgrims, but there are two other cars there, besides Lot's truck. One is a gray Lincoln no one recognizes. The other is Carter's Pontiac.

"Bless his heart," Aileen murmurs.

When they knock on the trailer door, though, no one answers. Finally, Nancy notices that the front door and front windows of the old Chastain place are open, and they all walk up the clay drive lined with crepe myrtles just past their prime.

Lot comes out on the porch just as they get to the front steps.

"My land," he says, "is it Christmas? Don't never see this much family." He smiles, and Nancy sees how it doesn't seem to go all the way up to his eyes.

Carter comes out, too, and right beside him is a light-skinned black woman.

"How do you do?" she says, walking quickly down the steps to greet Aileen, Sam and Nancy. She picks Wade right out of Nancy's arms as if she's known the child all his life, and he picks up on this and breaks out into a big smile.

"I'm Sebara Tatum," she tells them, when it's obvious that Lot isn't saying anything. "The Lord has brought me here."

"He drives a nice car," Carter says, and Sebara laughs as if she's just heard the funniest joke in the world.

Sebara, it turns out, has been cleaning. There are throw rugs with years of dust hanging on the clothesline whose posts miraculously haven't fallen down yet. The living room floor smells like ammonia.

"My sisters and I come here every month or so and clean," Aileen sniffs, although it's been almost two months now.

"Well," Sebara says, "there's cleaning and there's cleaning. I just thought we ought to air it out a little, is all."

"Want you all to hang around until the pilgrims get here," Lot says. "Might see something."

Carter says he's seen enough, and, when Sam says he thinks he'll stay awhile, Aileen asks Carter if he'll give her a ride.

"I reckon I've seen enough, too," she says, not saying good-bye to anyone.

"Did you get a look at that back bedroom?" Aileen asks Carter when they are out of the others' earshot.

"Yeah, I saw it," Carter says. "What about it?"

"The bed is made," Aileen said.

Carter shrugs. "Maybe Lot's planning to take in boarders."

Sam, Nancy and Wade go for a walk, following the old trail that leads around behind the barn and winds down to the river. The ruts are filled with water in places, so they have to walk in the middle, where the grass tickles their ankles. The woods close in just past the barn, and Nancy thinks to herself that she's glad she isn't here alone, even if Sam hasn't been much company today.

They walk past an old brick chimney, and then the woods open out again and they're behind the sawdust pile. It isn't smoking today, as if all the rain earlier in the week has doused it.

"It'll come back," Sam says. "It always does. One time, it quit for two or three months, except I guess it was burning inside somewhere. Then, suddenly one day, it started up again."

Wade is fascinated by the large orange mound, taller even than some of the trees around it, and he starts crying when his parents won't let him go play on it.

Past the sawdust pile, the road starts to dip sharply toward the river.

"That's the pond where that boy drowned," Sam says, pointing to his left, and Nancy holds more tightly to Wade's hand.

The trail gets more and more muddy, and at times it seems it is only there in Sam's memory. He has to persuade Nancy to continue, finally telling her that he's going on, and if she wants to return, she'll have to go by herself.

When they get to the river at last, it's more frightening to Nancy than the deserted trail. Three days of rain in the mountains have caused the normally placid August flow to turn into a flood. The water is out of its banks, a quarter of the way up the sycamores that are hugging the shore. Nancy sees what looks like a tree go crashing by in the brown torrent, and she and Sam have to shout to make themselves heard. Wade, sensing her fear, starts to cry.

"Wanna go home," the boy bawls, and his father picks him up impatiently.

"It's just the river," he says, but the boy continues to cry. Finally, Nancy takes him.

"Am I your buddy?" Sam says, loud enough for Nancy to hear.

Nancy feels herself blush. She turns and starts walking back uphill through the mud, hoping she's remembered the trail.

They return to the house, Nancy partly carrying, partly pulling Wade, while Sam walks by himself, 100 feet back. Once, she and the boy take a wrong turn, and Sam just says, "Left." She turns that way and finds the trail again.

By the time they get back, they see that Sebara and Lot

have been busy. They've taken one of the half whiskey barrels that Aileen and her sisters used to set out flowers in the yard, emptied the dirt from it, and have dragged it over by the barn. They put it in the middle of the area facing the fast-approaching appearance of Jesus-on-the-barn, where the clay has been pounded into a brick-like, flat surface smooth as a hardwood floor by several thousand shuffling feet.

Sebara has gone into Monacan and bought a can of red spray paint and some stencils. She's in the midst of making a sign on a piece of plywood that Lot has brought out of the barn. By the time Sam, Nancy and Wade have cleaned up and come outside, it's 6:45, almost time for the first pilgrims. Lot's gotten good at estimating when the light will strike the barn just right, and he figures it'll be about 7:30 tonight. When they come around the corner, they see the sign, nailed to a tree behind the whiskey barrel: FOR THE CHAPEL OF JESUS-ON-THE-BARN.

Sebara has disappeared for the moment. Lot sees his relatives looking at the bucket and the sign.

"I don't reckon this is fancy enough for the Baptists and Presbyterians and all in town," he says, giving that mocking smile that sends up storm warnings for everyone who knows him.

"It's fine, Uncle Lot," Sam says. "Everybody ought to worship their own way."

Lot's on the verge of a diatribe about religion when Sebara comes around the corner. She has on the red robe, and she's put on eye shadow and makeup. She has a Bible in her right hand.

"Don't you look pretty," Lot says.

"Mr. Chastain," she says to him, smiling, "you'll turn my head."

Sam, Nancy and Wade stay, and the pilgrims start arriving. They are mostly country people who've driven a long way. The men get out and stretch, leaning on their cars. The women take the children with them and get as close as they can get to the barn. They are mostly shy, but one or two ask Lot if it's his barn. Some of them seem suspicious of the black woman in the choir robe.

At about the time that the sun strikes the barn through

the trees, Sebara steps up on the stool she's put beside the whiskey barrel. She begins to speak, in the same sing-song voice that she uses for her congregation on Wednesdays and Sundays:

"And the LOOORRD looked down (pause) and he SAAIID to himself (pause) my PEOPLE have become sinners (pause) that COOOVET their neighbors' things (pause). I will SHOOOW them a sign (pause) that the WOOORD is still the word (pause) and the BLOOD of the lamb (pause) will NOOOT be mocked by men (pause). By the NAAIILS in my hands (pause) and the THORNS on my head (pause) I SIGNIFY to you (pause) that the DAAAAY is coming soon (pause) when the FIIRRST shall be last (pause) and the LAAAST shall be first."

While she talks, the sun does its magic, and the crowd lets out its breath in unison as the figure appears. It reminds Nancy of the reaction to a particularly good fireworks explosion at a Fourth of July celebration. Sebara's rhythmic speech, almost like a chant, has made it appear that she has brought Jesus here personally. Even Lot, who has seen the vision appear every night since April, murmurs to Sam, "Ain't that something?"

She's somehow timed her sermon so that it ends at just about the same time that the last light fades. She closes with an invitation:

"We will BUUIILD him a chapel (pause) to HONOR his coming (pause) to SHOOW our appreciation (pause) for his GOODNESS and mercy (pause) that the AANGEL of death (pause) might SPARE our souls (pause) when the ROOOLL is called. Amen."

She makes a waving gesture toward the sign and the bucket. People file by, offering mostly bills. A husband gets ready to put a dollar bill in and his wife grabs his hand and whispers to him. He reluctantly produces a five and drops it in instead.

"Praise Jesus," says Sebara Tatum.

In the fast-fading light, Sam, Nancy and the now-sleeping Wade wait a few minutes for the hundred or so cars to disperse.

"So," Nancy says to Sebara, "you intend to build a chapel here, through donations?"

Sebara lifts the robe over her head and gives it a shake. "Indeed we do," she says. "And we don't have much time. In a few more weeks, the sun won't even shine on the barn any more until spring. And who knows if Jesus is goin' to come back or not then?"

She leans against the side of Lot's truck to take off one of her high heels.

"Work," she says, looking up at Nancy and giving her a wink, "for the night is coming."

Since Lot returned at noon, with Sebara's Lincoln following close behind the familiar pickup truck, Billy Basset has been keeping a low profile. He needs to think.

He's seen the two of them working together to clean the old house, and he's seen the fixed bed in the back room. He knows his days of plundering silverware and silver dollars are over, at least for now. He came by in the afternoon, asking Lot if he needed any help. Lot said he didn't, not even thanking him for feeding Granger, and Sebara just looked at him, the kind of sizing-up look that Billy gets when he's buying an ounce from someone who doesn't know him.

Still, Billy feels as if the black woman might be on to something. He decides to stick around, half out of the profit motive and half out of curiosity.

He's in the back of the crowd, one of the few teen-agers there, when Sebara gives her first sermon at the barn, and he watches as people lay a coating of green on the bottom of the old whiskey barrel.

At dark, he goes back down to the river to camp out, not knowing when or if he'll be able to slip back into the big house again. He's eaten some beans and franks cooked on his Coleman stove, washing them down with a Budweiser from a six-pack he has cooling in the nearby river water, and is just lighting up a joint when the tent flap opens. It's Sebara.

"Lot said you stay here," she says to him.

"He said I could," Billy says, thinking he's about to be sent back across the river.

Sebara lifts the joint out of Billy's fingers and takes a toke

113

that makes the end of it glow bright red. Billy imagines he can see the only source of his evening's entertainment visibly shrinking.

Sebara finally lets out a cloud of blue smoke. It comes out both nostrils and her mouth, rising into the already hazy air inside the tent.

"Good stuff," she says as she looks around. "You ain't going to be able to stay here much longer. Be getting cold pretty soon."

"I'm going to Florida," Billy says, since it's the only place he can think of. He knows he's probably going back to his mother's.

Sebara squats down and leans close to him, looking at him straight on.

"I seen you," she says softly. "I see everything. You be hanging around the store, selling that stuff to the other little peckerheads. You ain't hanging out up here for your health, for sure."

She reaches in the pocket of the jeans she changed into after the crowd left and pulls out a small stub, a roach Billy knows he forgot to take with him when he was cleaning up one morning.

"Ought to be more careful," she says to him, and then: "How'd you like to have some cash in your pockets when you go to Florida, river boy? A lot of cash."

Billy looks up and sees a smile start to form on Sebara's face and feels one creeping onto his. A kindred spirit.

"Just be cool," she tells the boy. "I got to get back inside. Told the old fool I was going out to the car to get some stuff. He'll be wondering. But I got things for you to do, things that'll pay good. For you and me."

She slips out of the tent. Later, Billy goes outside, stoned, and lies on the ground. He's happy that the familiar burning smell of the sawdust pile is missing, although it did keep the mosquitoes away. A shooting star flashes past almost horizontal to the ground. Billy thinks it's a sign.

CHAPTER EIGHTEEN

Nancy feels that she and Sam are walking on eggshells, and she's hoping it will all resolve itself. She realizes she's a coward. Although she visibly flinches every time Wade says "Buddy," she's not sure what she wants to do.

Sam is spending more time at the Civitan Club, often not coming home until Nancy's already asleep, his exaggerated attempts at tiptoeing making every board in the old house creak. If he had come in riding a pogo stick, he couldn't have awakened her more thoroughly, Nancy thinks more than once.

And he seems to be getting more obsessed with his dream of dunking a basketball. He's spending more and more time working out; he's gone in the mornings, even Sundays now. Still, when Nancy asks how he's doing, he's evasive, says he's not ready yet, that he has a ways to go before he can actually get far enough above the rim to dunk. He claims he's still losing weight, but Nancy can't really notice any improvement there. It would be easier, he tells her, if only his hands were large enough to palm the ball while he jumped.

They haven't made love during the week after their tryst in the front seat at the drive-in, and Nancy is starting to think maybe she imagined it, that it was something she dreamed up for a character in the novel she's writing.

On a Saturday afternoon in mid-September, Nancy takes Wade and goes to visit her family in Richmond. Sam is spending the whole day at a pig-picking his club is holding, keeping watch over the skewered animal as it cooks all morning and part of the afternoon, drinking a beer every hour, then every half-hour. Nancy figures this will be a good time to go see her parents.

She never makes plans to call Buddy or see him, but it's as if something pulls her off the road on a second's notice when she sees a pay phone booth, and before she knows it, she's calling the now-familiar number, but no one answers. She gets back in the car, both disappointed and mildly relieved that she's been saved from herself.

When she gets to Suzanne and Pat's, she sees that Candy's car is in the driveway, along with another one that seems vaguely familiar.

She still has the key to her parents' front door, and she always just lets herself in. Everyone seems to be on the back porch, from the noise, so she goes back there, leading Wade, who hangs on to two of her fingers and keeps saying, "Grandpa, Grandpa."

Suzanne comes around the corner and greets them both, but she has a worried look on her face and blocks Nancy's access to the porch, where the noise has suddenly died.

"I told Pat we ought to have asked you about this beforehand," she says. "But he said it'd been so long ago, that it wouldn't matter."

While she talks and Nancy tries to figure out the bottom line, Wade wanders out on the porch where he sees his grandfather and his Aunt Candy and his Aunt Marilou. Better yet, he sees another familiar human being sitting beside Aunt Marilou, holding her hand.

"Buddy!" he exclaims.

"I see you all have already met," Marilou says dryly to Buddy Molloy.

It turns out that Buddy has been dating Marilou for a month now, but that everyone in the O'Neil family has kept it from Nancy. "We just didn't want to ruffle feathers, honey," Suzanne tells her.

With only seven people present, it's impossible to keep Nancy and Buddy away from each other completely, and it makes things so awkward that Suzanne finally exclaims, while they're all sitting together at the picnic table outside over hot dogs and hamburgers, "Would you all stop? Would everybody just act natural? You're making me as nervous as a whore in church with a bastard on each knee."

Everyone except Nancy laughs. She leaves the picnic table,

and Buddy follows her. He catches up in the old bedroom that Nancy shared with Marilou when they were growing up.

"I didn't mean to," he tells her as she slaps his hand from around her shoulder. "If I'd have known what it would lead to. . . . She just looks so much like you."

"How many more times were you going to fuck me before you told me?" she spits out.

"I ran into her at the mall one day," he says. "We talked for half an hour. Before I knew what I was doing, I asked her out."

"And she said yes?"

"She thinks we haven't seen each other in years . . . or at least she did."

Buddy puts his hand lightly on her shoulder, and she lets him leave it there this time.

"I know we can't get back together," he says, almost whispering. "Ever since the reunion, though, I've been thinking about you. Before then, too. But then it got really bad. And Marilou is so much like you. It's like a chance not to screw it up this time."

"And what about me? Have I had my chance?"

Buddy doesn't say anything, can't think of anything to make it any better.

Nancy goes back outside, tells Marilou it's all right, then walks over and throws up on one of her father's prize rosebushes.

"Well, Wade," she tells the boy on the way back to Monacan, "it looks like it's just you and me. No more Buddy."

"No Buddy?" the child asks. He never says the name again.

Nancy is working on her novel the next day when Carter comes by. Wade's asleep, and Sam is gone, dressed to run another endless series of hundred-yard dashes. The secret, he has told Nancy, is in converting horizontal speed into vertical speed; the faster you run, the higher you jump.

Since she and her family moved to Monacan, Nancy has written almost 100 pages. Over the months, she's built a story around characters that are obviously styled after Buddy and Lot, although it hurts her to think of the former right now. The story is about a father who has been committed to a mental institution and his divorced son who gets him out and with whom he is living. Nancy is repulsed by Lot the person but fascinated by Lot the character, and she feels she must get as much of Lot's character as possible into the story if it's going to succeed.

Nancy treasures the few moments each day when she can write undisturbed, and she feels guilty over her annoyance when Wade's first incoherent words tell her he'll be crying for her in a few minutes, or when a knock on the door announces some neighbor who has come to visit.

She's only been writing for half an hour when she hears the front doorbell. She curses under her breath softly and hopes Wade won't wake up. Carter is standing there, holding a grocery bag full of tomatoes. He acts embarrassed to be intruding even on his son's family. Nancy likes her father-in-law and tries to make him feel welcome whenever he visits.

"Last ones we'll get this year," he says, handing her the bag. "We've got more than we know what to do with. Thought you all might want some."

Nancy has been secretly throwing out vegetables all summer. Carter and Marie share the bounty of their half-acre garden, and Sam and Nancy's neighbors will often leave bags of peas or okra or sometimes a watermelon on the porch. The fact that Sam and Nancy don't have a garden themselves and thus can't reciprocate only makes everyone more eager to share. Sam has suggested more than once that Nancy learn how to can vegetables so they don't spoil before they can be eaten. As with the suggestion that she work at the drugstore, Nancy puts him off with vague promises. She can't imagine spending the time she sees Sam's mother spend on preserving food as long as there are grocery stores.

Nancy invites Carter in. She doesn't tell him that Sam's out, because if she does, he'll probably mumble something about having to get back home, and, despite the loss of free time, she enjoys Carter's visits.

She goes into the kitchen to get them a couple of Cokes, spilling the sticky liquid down the sides of their glasses as she tries to fill them too quickly around the ice cubes inside.

Carter leans against the kitchen door sill, watching her.

"Don't have to use all that ice for me," he says, as if there's a shortage.

He sits at the kitchen table, looking incongruous in the knit shirt and baggy pants that they bought for him at Christmas. In spite of his college degree and penchant for Faulkner and Thomas Wolfe, Nancy always thinks of Carter as a farmer who somehow got sidetracked into pharmacy. His hands are hardened as a brick-layer's from spending much of his "free" time in the yard and garden. He has a tan that stops at the nape of his neck.

"How are Lot and Sebara doing?" she asks him. He gives her a curious look and then shakes his head.

"Lot's a sick man, has been a long time," Carter says, sighing. "I don't know what's going to come of all this." He's been out to Old Monacan again, a week after Sebara first appeared, and it seems to him that the chance to give money has actually increased the size of the crowds at Lot's barn. He's seen people putting multiple bills into Sebara's whiskey barrel, and he's seen the Basset boy, who Sheriff Burden says is probably messed up in drugs, standing back from the crowd like a dog waiting for scraps.

It doesn't bother Carter, or at least it doesn't bother him as much as it does the girls and Marie, that Lot appears to be living with a black woman, in their parents' old house. Carter or anyone can see that it's the big house and not the trailer that is being used for human habitation now, and Sebara Tatum's Lincoln seems to be a permanent fixture. They use Lot's truck when they go for groceries or supplies.

What does worry him is Lot himself. When Lot gets excited about something, and it doesn't work out, he has the worst of his "spells." Carter would like to tell Sebara Tatum or even the Basset boy this, but he doesn't know how.

"Has Lot always been like he is now?" Nancy asks Carter, who isn't used to being asked such questions. In the family, Lot is like the thunderstorms that can come eight afternoons in a row, then not be seen for a month. Lot is a force of nature. With outsiders, Carter doesn't usually talk about his older brother.

"Momma said he was colicky when he was little," he says after a long silence. "I remember that she would cook special

119

things for him because he couldn't—or wouldn't—eat what everybody else was eating. He'd wash his hands like he was a doctor fixing to operate, and he couldn't bear to have any of his food mixed together. He'd pile up little servings of peas and corn and put a piece of ham or chicken 'way on the other side of the plate, and better not any of the juice from the corn touch the peas or the chicken. I reckon Momma spoiled him too much."

"That's funny," Nancy says. "With him being the oldest and all," but Carter tells her that Warren, the one who died in the war, was a year older.

"Holly was the baby," he says, taking off his bifocals and wiping them on the front of his knit shirt. "She was spoiled too. Everybody took to her. Momma spoiled Lot, but everybody spoiled Holly. She had curly yellow hair and she always seemed like she was happy. Even Lot was nice around her. He didn't make her tempt the devil like he did the rest of us. Lot was full of meanness."

He sees Nancy's puzzlement and explains about the other sawdust pile, the one that finally burned when he was a boy, and about the game they all played.

"Warren made it up," he says, "but Warren didn't ever make any of the girls run over it like Lot did."

He goes quiet, thinking about the first time his older brother made him scale the big orange hill of smoke. The burning cinders made his eyes water, and Lot slapped him roughly with his open hand across the back of his head, telling him not to be a baby, telling him that he'd beat him good if he didn't start running across the hill and beat him worse if he told their father.

Carter remembers but doesn't tell about the uproar and the shame when Holly had to go live with the Bondurants when she was only 10 years old, how she didn't come back home for good until she was 16 and then just for her last year of high school, how she had turned into a nail-biter, a jumper at sudden sounds, a crier.

He remembers but doesn't tell about the day the men in uniforms came to get Lot for the Army, how nobody would tell where Lot was, claiming he was working in North Carolina. How the sergeant took him off to one side, him 15 years old, and told him he'd be drafted some day soon and they'd remember who he was if he didn't tell them where his brother was hiding.

How the sergeant looked at him real close and said, You the one that sent the note, ain't you, boy? You don't have to say nothing, son, just nod your head. And how, when the sergeant, his breath close enough to smell breakfast, asked, Is he hiding back there in the woods? Carter nodded so slightly that he wasn't sure the sergeant saw him. They brought Lot out less than an hour later, in handcuffs, and took him off. Lot seemed to look right at him, Carter remembers, on the way to the car, like they told him who it was that turned him in. But by the time Lot got out of the Army, Carter was gone from home, working in Richmond and saving for college, and nobody, not even his mother, seemed to think that Carter Chastain had turned his own brother in to the draft board.

It comes back to Carter in a rush that he had prayed for his brother not to return from the war. It comes back to him how, when Warren, the good one, was killed instead, it seemed like God was showing him what could and could not be prayed for. They caught Carter trying to enlist when he was 16, down at courthouse square where everybody knew how old everybody else's children were. All the men thought young Carter was a pistol, full of piss and vinegar, for wanting to go off and kill Huns when he wasn't even through high school. But all Carter wanted to do was be punished. After the war he was too young to fight in, after he'd gone to pharmacy school and come back to live in Monacan, he tried to look after Lot because he had wished and prayed him dead.

All of this, all that business with Holly and Lot and the day they took Lot away, but not for good, these are not for talking about, Carter knows, not even with your daughter-in-law.

"Lot's just full of meanness," he says as he finishes his Coke and rises from the kitchen chair. "Stay away from him if you can."

NOW

CHAPTER NINETEEN

One morning in late May, when a spring shower has chased the other ragged park regulars inside, where they must pretend to read and not fall asleep, Nancy finds Sebara hovering by the back door, pressed into a corner away from the rain. She still has on Nancy's old red dress. She looks as if she's losing weight.

Nancy coaxes her inside and leads her to an empty table at the back of the reference section. Sebara sets her bag on the middle of the table, and Nancy sits across from her, but not far enough away not to almost gag from the smell.

"Sebara," Nancy asks the other woman when it looks as if she's about to nod off, "what happened? At Lot's, I mean. I never did know all of it."

Sebara is silent for half a minute, and Nancy thinks that she's too far gone to even remember that far back. Then the old woman starts to chuckle to herself.

"Don't reckon it matters who knows now," she says, not bothering to hold her hand over her mouth while she hacks and wheezes.

"You see," she says, when she catches her breath, "I had me this plan. I always wanted to live in Florida . . ."

Sebara tells Nancy her story, filling in all the blanks that Nancy couldn't figure out for herself from what she'd seen that night, what the Chastains knew and what the newspaper reported. She tells Nancy about changing her name and about how she never spoke to another soul from Virginia until she came back, "broke as a convict," three years ago.

"I had it made in the shade there," she tells Nancy. "Had money in the bank, had a maid come in once a week and clean. Wasn't but two miles from the ocean. Went there every day.

"But I got lonesome there, lonesome for preaching, lonesome for folks clapping their hands and shouting. So I went to Belle Glade, because a man told me they was bad to have revivals in Belle Glade.

"And he was right. They just eat Jesus up in that town. One night I took in $20,000. $20,000! They had me on television, and I was scared somebody'd see me up here.

"But Belle Glade won't on no ocean; it was in the swamp. Lord, it was hot there! And then I got to doing that cocaine." Sebara shakes her head. "Then I don't know where all that money went to. I finally got a job right on the ocean," she goes on, with a bitter smile. "I was a maid, working for some rich folks in Palm Beach. But they said I stole. You know something? They was right." She laughs out loud, and a man in a suit two tables away looks up, annoyed.

Sebara's laugh turns into a coughing fit. Finally, she goes on with her story.

"I had to leave Florida," she says, "and I was damn happy to. But I been in jail in Macon, Georgia, and Bennettsville, South Carolina, and I don't know where all else.

"You know what's the blessed truth, though? When I was preachin' up here, it wasn't nothing but a way to put food on the table. Folks is always happy to give their money to a preacher, seems like.

"Now, though, I done used all that up, and it seems like maybe they is something there. Like I could of done something big, bigger than enough money to take me to Florida. Sometimes I dreams about that barn, and Jesus on it. But you know what's funny? I never for sure could see Him on there. I mean, I'd see the shadows and the scratches in the wood and how they come together, but I never did believe any of that stuff."

Sebara scratches herself and picks at her nose.

"Now, though," she says, "I think there was something up there, and Jesus put a curse on me. I been cursed for 20 years."

Nancy tries to give Sebara five dollars for telling her the story, but Sebara pushes it back.

"I promised Jesus," she says, holding her head up and looking dead on at Nancy for the first time with the red-and-yellow eyes, "that I wouldn't never take no more money from nobody, till He calls me to be with Him. I eats at the shelter, sleeps there when I can. I gets food from strangers sometimes, 'cause I don't think even Jesus would 'grudge me that. But I can't take no more money, or I'll go to hell sure as I'm sitting here. It was money that brought me down. If I hadn't had all that money, I couldn't of bought that cocaine."

Nancy notices that Sebara never even asks about what happened to Billy Basset and Lot after she left. Maybe, she thinks, Sebara read about it in a Florida newspaper.

A month later, the day after Nancy finishes the novel that doesn't come home, she is five minutes late for work because of an accident in front of the parking deck.

When she comes in, she tells Doris Ann Potts, the fat woman who works with her in reference, why she's late.

Doris Ann doesn't look up, just says, "Oh, the ambulance must have been for the old woman, the one that stays in the park. Walked right in front of a bus, I heard. Good riddance. She was nasty."

1971

CHAPTER TWENTY

*S*ebara *gets up at night sometimes and walks. She thinks I'm asleep, but I don't sleep easy. Never have. I go to sleep, I start having one of them dreams, one of the bad ones, and then I wake up and just lie there. Must make a fuss when I have 'em, because when I woke up the other night, Sebara was stroking my forehead and telling me it was all right.*

I seen her out the window up here. She'll walk down to her car and then go off into the woods, down towards the river. Don't have no flashlight or nothing. She'll be gone an hour sometimes, then come slip back in beside me. I started to ask her where she'd been last night, but then she got all lovey-dovey with me and it made me forget all about it. Reckon everybody's got to be by theirself once in a while.

They're after us now. Fire chief come by Wednesday, said he was going to shut us down on account of the sawdust pile. I told him won't none of his business, and he said it was because of all the people coming out here to see Jesus. Like they might catch fire or something. I told him he better keep away from here.

Next day, which was yesterday, them folks from the historical society come by, still a-trying to get me to sell 'em my house and land. I just laughed at 'em, said they better get in line. They looked right puzzled, so I told them that my brother and sisters thought they were going to sell it all to some developer, and the fire chief thought he was going to come here and walk all over me because I won't put out a damn fire in a goddamn sawdust pile, but that they was all wrong, and so are you, I told them. Said, me and Sebara is going to stay right here and build us a chapel to honor the appearance of the Lord Jesus Christ.

And then I run 'em off.

Sebara was gone both times. She takes the money into town, puts it in an account me and her have now at the Virginia National

131

Bank there. She showed me the bank book; we've got near-bout $25,000 already, just donations from folks that come to the barn. I went with her when she opened it, and the girl frowned and went and got her boss. He come over all smiles and slicked-back hair when he won't nothing but Arthur Dillon's boy that was too lazy to work. Reckon that girl hadn't never seen a white man and a colored woman open a bank account before.

But the sun is setting earlier and earlier. Sebara says that she figures we got three more weeks that it'll hit the barn enough to let 'em see Jesus, so we got to make hay while the sun shines, like she says.

She even got a man from Channel 6 and one from the Times-Dispatch, *with a photographer, out here, and so now everybody knows we're coming up to what Sebara calls the grand finale. Then, we'll take the money and start building a shrine here, right on the other side of the barn. Sebara says they can lay the foundation this fall, and then we can raise enough money in the spring, when Jesus comes back, to build the rest next summer.*

She's a smart woman. She's got hundreds and hundreds coming out here every night now. They got to line up and go by single-file so everybody can see it for a minute or two. Sometimes folks will just fall to their knees when they see it, and we have to pick them up and move them along. The Basset boy helps us do that.

Sometimes I wonder what Momma and Daddy must think about all of this. Yesterday, I went over to Egypt. The pines are all grown now and being pushed out by the white oaks, but there's still a place in the middle there, mine and Holly's place. I go there sometimes when it seems like things is moving too fast. Sometimes, it seems like I can hear Momma talking when the wind is blowing from the west.

Yesterday, it seemed like she said to me, "Don't never leave; Don't never leave."

It gets hard for me to tell, sometimes, what's the wind and what's real. I'll have the fat lightning dream and wake up gnawing my pillow, Sebara telling me it's all right.

And then I wonder if Sebara ain't a dream, too.

CHAPTER TWENTY-ONE

Sebara picks up Billy between Jeter's house and the state highway, as they'd planned. He steps out of the cornfield, startling the black woman for a second. He throws down the cigarette he's been smoking among the bone-dry, waiting-to-be-tilled stalks and gets into the Lincoln.

At the state road, they turn left and head north. Billy can see the top of the courthouse and the water tower off to the right, seemingly suspended in air above the early October oaks, just now turning.

They're headed for Murro.

Billy eyes the brown deposit bag between them on the front seat.

Sebara eyes him.

"Makes the old fool think it's on the up-and-up if I leave with all the money in a O-fficial bank bag," she says, laughing and speaking in the exaggerated black accent she uses to con white people. Billy's in on the joke, though, for now. "He sure is goin' to be surprised when he tries to draw out of that account."

Sebara Tatum became minister of the Ebenezer Free Will Gospel Holiness Church because her father was the minister before her, and because she learned well.

Lucas Tatum founded the church and named it. He was a roofer whose men covered most of the houses and stores in the black communities of Moseby County. One hot July day, when the shingles on the roof didn't seem as if they could be much hotter than the tar in the buckets the men carried up with them, Lucas Tatum stepped off the roof of Bessie McAdams' two-story house and had a vision.

Lucas hadn't meant to step off the roof that day. He didn't

133

usually go up on the roof himself except to see how the job was progressing, but he was helping out because his crew was a man short. He was working alongside an apprentice, a boy just 15 years old, all arms and legs and thumbs. When the boy stepped back near the highest point on the roof, forgetting where he was, he kicked the tar bucket over not five feet from where Lucas Tatum was half-sitting, half-squatting, looking the other way. The tar stuck to his right arm like napalm and burned through his right pants leg.

The other men on the crew said that Lucas didn't scream, just got up and took the three steps it took to reach the side of the house, 25 feet off the ground. Then he took a fourth step.

He fell into the forsythia bushes next to Bessie McAdams' oil tank. The first man who got to him said that Lucas kept saying the same thing over and over: "Praise Jesus, I'm alive. Praise Jesus, I'm alive."

Lucas Tatum became convinced that he was the beneficiary of a miracle. He had suffered burns over large areas of the right side of his body, and he would always walk with a limp afterward, but Lucas was sure that, if he hadn't heeded the voice that told him to jump off the side of the house, he would have died.

"I was going to jump somewhere," he explained to his wife later. "What most people would've done would be just slide down the roof like a bag of shingles and fall off, and then where would I have been? I'd of busted myself wide open on Bessie McAdams' concrete driveway.

"But that voice, it told me, 'Walk off the side of the roof.' And I must of hit the only place I could of jumped where I'd be saved by a nice, soft forsythia bush. Plus, the fall shook some of the tar off. I'd of been kilt if I hadn't minded that voice."

No one else in Lucas' family felt he or they were especially lucky. While he was in the hospital, his business went broke without him to run it, and that plus the hospital bills cost the Tatums their house. Lucas and his wife and five children had to go live with his parents.

But Lucas Tatum never wavered in his plans for the rest of his life. As soon as he was able to get around with a cane, he paid a visit to an elder in the Murro Baptist Church, the white church that had just, a year before, moved into its new building and abandoned the wood structure that had served as its sanctuary since the Civil War.

The Baptists had planned to sell the old building for scrap lumber, but Lucas persuaded them to rent it to him for his as-yet-invisible congregation.

Within a year, Lucas Tatum's church, which he named the Ebenezer Free Will Gospel Holiness Church and which was part of no denomination, had grown to 50 members and was challenging the AME Zion church five miles away for black souls. Its main attraction, other than Lucas' zeal, was that it always had a good roof.

The Tatums themselves moved into the back of a store that Lucas' wife ran to help pay the bills. As soon as their children got old enough to get jobs, they left, disenchanted by church services five nights a week plus Sundays, unhappy over the beatings their father administered when they failed to memorize a Bible verse every day.

Sebara was the exception. She was only a year old when Lucas walked off Bessie McAdams' roof. She was eight years younger than her nearest sibling, and the challenging life of her father's church was all she'd ever known.

She was a beautiful child, all the church's members agreed. They'd seen her at six as the Virgin Mary in the Christmas pageant, at nine singing gospel solos, at 12 preaching her first youth sermon, at 15 taking over occasionally for her ailing father, who was dead of a heart attack before Sebara graduated from high school. Sebara's mother had already been dead five years, and the fourth of her siblings had left their store-house four years before that.

Sebara felt she had no choice. At 17, she took over her father's church. She lived by herself in the now-defunct store and persuaded the board of deacons to pay her meager rent.

For 12 years, she preached to the congregation of her father's former church. Some of the older members didn't like her flashy ways, preferring the earnest poverty Lucas Tatum had exhibited. They didn't like the way she traded cars every other year, always trading up.

But Sebara Tatum made the church grow. People would

135

come from miles around to hear her preach, and they were entranced by the way she would half-preach, half-sing at them.

But what nobody knew, because Sebara kept her own counsel, was that she was tired, tired deep in her bones, of the Ebenezer Free Will Gospel Holiness Church and all its members.

Ever since she was a small child, Sebara had been amazed by the gullibility of the church-goers. She saw that anyone who was willing to scream and chant and allege to speak in tongues was heeded. She realized that the mere claim that one had received divine instruction was enough to convince most of the church's members. Sebara learned well and put it all to use when it came her turn to be its minister.

There was a meeting, attended by most of the church's members, on a Tuesday night two weeks after her father's death. The subject was Lucas Tatum's successor. While some of the members, including two of her father's former deacons, felt that Sebara should take over the church's leadership, many in attendance wanted to bring in an experienced, older minister from outside.

Sebara arrived at the last minute, dressed in a long red dress, and walked to the front of the church, ascended to the pulpit and looked over to her best friend, Marva Coleman, the organist. The first and only order of business was supposed to be a discussion of the church's choice for its new minister. But Sebara soon made it known that she had her own agenda.

"The LOOORRRD be with you," she said, and Marva Coleman hit a note on the organ. The crowd stirred.

"I have COME with the word,
"God's HOOOLLY word,
"That He SEEENNNT to old Abraham,
"And He PASSED to the prophets,
"That He gave the LOOORRD Jesus,
"That's still LIVING today,
"The SAAAME holy word,
"That LED Lucas Tatum,
"To FORESAKE his earthly goods,
"And FOUND this church,

"With the LOOORD Jesus as its cornerstone,
"Didn't need NO OTHER cornerstone."

Sebara, alternately singing and preaching, would pause every few words and Marva Coleman would punctuate the words with a blast from the organ. The audience swayed and moaned, under the spell of her chant. None of the deacons was brave enough to tell a 17-year-old girl she was out of order.

"The LOOORD came to me," she continued,
"And He TOOOK me by the hand,
"And He SAAIIID to me, 'Child,
"You must FORESAKE your youth
"And TAKE UP the yoke,
"For your FAAATHER'S work
"Is not yet DOOONE.'"

Sebara went on for 45 minutes, and at the end of the 45 minutes, there was no vote and no discussion. Two old women and a child fainted, and many fell into the aisles and spoke in tongues. The church was hers.

Sebara Tatum is 29 years old now. For the last eight years, she's been slipping enough money out of the collection plate to save a few thousand dollars. When she first heard about Lot Chastain's barn and the vision on it, she didn't think of it beyond its possibilities as an interesting change of venue for the Wednesday night prayer group.

But once she saw what the pilgrims believed was the outline of Jesus on the old wall, she knew that there was a plan. Not necessarily Jesus' plan, but a plan nonetheless.

She's included Billy in her scheme because Billy is everywhere, and he is, she can see, a natural criminal, one who would always smell out the larceny in neighboring hearts. Better, she thinks, to be up-front about it from the beginning. Or at least make Billy think she's up-front. Better to have him inside pissing out than outside pissing in.

They go along without speaking. Sebara turns left again beyond the river and passes the Ebenezer church. Sebara has handed over the church duties, other than the Sunday services, to Marva Coleman while she attends to matters at Lot's barn.

She turns in at her converted home, parking the big car

parallel to the side of the cinder-block building. She and Billy go inside and Sebara puts the money in the safe that sits in her bedroom, along with the rest.

"Must be almost $40,000 by now," Billy says, not taking his eyes off the stacks of green.

"Be a lot more than that by Saturday night," she tells the boy. "Folks will be taking out second mortgages to put old Jesus-on-the-barn over the top."

She's put out the word, through the TV and newspaper interviews, that she and Lot hope to have $75,000 after the Friday and Saturday sessions. They've brought in several hundred folding chairs, and Sebara has enlisted four Ebenezer church members to go around taking up the collection. The last hay crop of the year has been gathered by the man who rents what's left of the Chastain farmland, leaving the pilgrims with an almost unlimited parking lot. The weather report is for no rain through the weekend.

"Then," she tells Billy as she relocks the safe, "late Saturday night, when old Lot is asleep, you and me will meet outside at midnight, you'll dig up the strongbox and I'll come by here and unlock the safe, and we'll be in Florida by morning."

She's careful to keep the combination from Billy.

"Come on now, sweet boy," she tells him, grabbing him by a belt loop. "Time to give Momma some sugar."

CHAPTER TWENTY-TWO

Sam's going to the Outer Banks for a deep-sea fishing trip with several of his friends. He's bought all the equipment he's been told he'll need, and now, on Friday afternoon, he's home packing.

"Don't forget the Dramamine," Nancy reminds him.

"I don't get seasick," he tells her with his back turned, and she doesn't bother to remind him again about the honeymoon cruise.

The second week in October has been a quiet one for Sam and Nancy. He's been trying to get caught up at work so he won't have to miss the fishing trip; she's been trying to figure out what to do with the rest of her life.

"Can we talk?" she asks him, staring at his back.

He seems to stiffen slightly, still packing things into his bag. "About what?"

"About us. About not talking. You know, everything."

Sam still doesn't want to give up his holiday mood. Why, he wonders, can't this wait?

He sighs. "OK. Talk."

"What do you think's been going on?" she asks him.

"What do you mean?"

Nancy wonders if he's being obtuse on purpose.

"I mean," she says, "if you suspect me of doing something, I wish you'd tell me, instead of just slipping around here like I've got some social disease. I haven't had but two goddamn marriages, but this sure doesn't seem like the way one should work. Or am I wrong?"

Sam finally gives up on the packing and sits on their bed, facing Nancy. His face is turning red, she notices.

"I don't suspect you of anything," he says. "Why should I suspect you of anything? Do you suspect me of anything?"

It hasn't occurred to Nancy to suspect Sam of anything other than neglect.

"No. Should I?"

Sam starts to say something, even opens his mouth, then closes it.

"Should I?" Nancy repeats.

Sam hangs his head. "I thought you knew. I thought you must have known."

"What?" Nancy looks closely at Sam, who is avoiding her eyes. It's so quiet she can hear Wade breathing as he sleeps in the next room. She figures she probably knows what, wonders why she didn't figure it out for herself before this.

So he tells her why he seems to be gaining back the weight he lost during the summer, despite working out every day, why he doesn't talk any more about how close he's getting to what he used to call critical mass, where he can dunk a basketball.

He tells her about Corinne Cobb DeVault.

Sam ran into Corinne again, in early August. He had just finished the 10 100-yard dashes that were part of his regimen for that day and was walking around the track, catching his breath, when a woman in a sweatsuit jogged toward him. It was Corinne, wet dream of his youth.

She acted as if she didn't even remember that she'd last seen him wrestling with a box of super tampons in the aisle at DrugLand, and she seemed glad to see him. Sam remembered, though, that Corinne's special talent, even in high school, was always seeming to be glad to see everyone, a fact he soon forgot.

She was married to the Mosby football coach, an ex-Virginia Tech linebacker from Baltimore whom Sam had met at the drugstore shortly after he moved back. Corinne had persuaded her husband to apply for the Mosby job so she could return to her home town. He'd given up a job at a larger school to take it. Sam remembered Frank DeVault from their meeting at the store as a fireplug, a man with no shoulders and an enormous gut, and he thought he must not have weighed so much when Corinne married him. Later, she would tell Sam that she'd married him because he intercepted a pass to beat Virginia her senior year.

Sam and Corinne talked, and he found out she usually worked out later in the day. Sam told her he had to come out early in order to get to the drugstore on time. The next morning, when Sam got to the track at his usual time, Corinne was there already.

Sam would run his dashes, going from one end zone to another. He hadn't been big enough or agile enough to play football in high school, and he liked to fantasize crossing the goal line with the winning touchdown against Lunenburg or Fluvanna. The only lines he crossed athletically at Mosby High were the ones used to mark the end of the one-mile run in track, and the cheerleaders had better things to do than scream for such as that.

In those days, while Corinne was leading cheers along the sideline and her boyfriend, Freddie Stone, was dismembering quarterbacks and halfbacks out on the field, Sam, along with a couple of bookish, smallish friends, would watch from the stands. They always called Corinne's boyfriend Fred Flintstone, behind his back of course. One of the highlights of Sam's junior and senior years was getting to drive a new Ford convertible through the goalposts at halftime of the homecoming game with a would-be queen atop the back seat. All the girls' boyfriends, of course, were in the locker room being called piss-ants by Coach Van Lear.

His senior year, he got to drive Corinne Cobb, who was already Miss Mosby High and head cheerleader. As part of the college-bound minority, they had some classes together, and Corinne had personally asked him to be her driver.

As he helped her into the car in the darkness behind the end zone, she grabbed his arm.

"Kiss me for luck?" she asked him. Their lips barely touched, because Corinne certainly didn't want to appear before her adoring fans—hers until the football team came back out—with smudged lipstick. She produced a Kleenex from somewhere and wiped the red from Sam's face.

"There," she'd said. "Now, let's go get 'em." Sam felt he was the recipient of a pep talk, but he never forgot that kiss.

Now, Corinne was accessible, and Sam was willing. Their workouts would end with a quick walking lap around the track, and they'd talk about old friends and their lives growing up in Monacan. Sam hadn't known Corinne well at all when they were teen-agers, and he was regretful to hear her claim she wasn't nearly as secure as she seemed back then, that she only went steady with Freddie Stone because she was afraid she'd be home alone on Fridays and Saturdays if she didn't go steady with someone.

One morning, Corinne told Sam that she wouldn't be able to jog at the field for the next two weeks.

"Why?" Sam asked her, disappointed.

She looked at him as if he'd just landed from Mars.

"Summer football drills, silly," she said. "You remember."

Sam didn't, mainly because he'd never played football, a fact he didn't bring up.

It turned out that Corinne's husband was starting preseason football practice the next day, so the field would be occupied from 6 a.m. until 9:30 a.m.

"Frank's so into it that he's going to put up a tent next to the field," she told Sam, "and stay out here all day. His assistants, too. He says the boys have got to understand that he can be tougher than them."

The team would have two practices a day, the last one ending after 8 p.m. Then, Frank and his assistants would spend another hour talking strategy and playing cards before they came home to their wives.

"I don't suppose I'll see much of old Frank the next two weeks," she sighed.

She had told Sam earlier that she and Frank had decided to wait to have children.

"What the hell, we're only 32. That's young," she'd said at the time.

Sam felt as if somebody had handed him a script, that all he had to do was read it properly to make things fall into place.

"I guess we'll have to figure out somewhere else to go, then," he said.

Corinne didn't miss her cue.

"Why don't you come over to the house tomorrow morning?" she said. "We can jog or something."

The next morning, Sam left home at the usual time, dressed in his shorts and T-shirt, but he kept going, right past the field where he could see teen-agers running endless laps and hear the bark of a high school coach pretending to be a drill instructor.

When he got to Corinne's house, a red brick rancher just outside town on a dead-end road, a quarter-mile from its nearest neighbor, Corinne answered the door. She was wearing pink jogging shorts and a gray T-shirt. She asked Sam if he'd like a cup of coffee. He and Corinne, girl of his dreams, sat in the kitchen, she on the window seat, he in a chair to her right. He could see the sun shining through the skylight on her hair, and he could catch the few slivers of gray that were just now beginning to interrupt all that blondeness. It would be years before they would speak loudly enough to suggest that Corinne Cobb DeVault was past her prime, but the sight of them moved Sam as nothing had in years.

"I've never forgotten that kiss you gave me at homecoming," he said, not planning to say such a thing at all.

She got up from the window seat and walked over to where Sam sat, his coffee cup still in his hand, leaned over and kissed him.

"Don't have to worry about smudging my lipstick any more," she said.

For the next two weeks, Sam didn't come home to shower after his workout. He didn't work out at all, except at Corinne's. He told Nancy that he could save time by showering at the gym, then grabbing a bite at the drugstore counter.

After Frank DeVault packed up his tent and ended two-a-days, Sam and Corinne arranged to meet twice a week at the new Holiday Inn out by the interstate, far enough away from town to make discovery a long shot. They'd meet at different times. Sam still made enough home deliveries, an indulgence he'd grudgingly inherited from his father's regime, to mask a 90-minute or two-hour disappearance.

Sam had almost come to see his dalliances as a normal and permanent part of his life. He didn't really think that Corinne was going to leave her husband, and he was reasonably certain that he wasn't going to leave Nancy and Wade. He wasn't even that star-struck any more. He was reasonably sure he didn't love Corinne, and he realized that sex with her was neither better nor worse than sex with Nancy, once the novelty wore off. There were things about Corinne that even put him off, which depressed him greatly. If 90 minutes at the Holiday Inn with Corinne Cobb, girl of his dreams, she not even bothering to wear panties, or, better yet, bothering to buy and wear crotchless ones, wasn't enough, what was?

But Corinne, he discovered, had bad breath, something that had escaped his attention 15 years before, and her habit of using the toilet while he was showering or shaving offended his sense of privacy. And, he came to realize, Corinne's conversations tended to always look backward. Other than the past, her only other interest seemed to be real estate, a vocation she was pursuing with some force on weekends. Her ability to mix business and pleasure sometimes stunned Sam. Once, riding him on the queen-sized motel bed, she stopped and asked him if he and Nancy were planning to rent forever.

But Sam had no plans to sever this link with the past he never had, just assumed that something would happen. He actually had to admit that he felt worse about quitting his quest for the ultimate vertical leap than he did about cheating on Nancy. Every time he drove by the weight room or the high school track, he felt a pang.

And Sam hadn't meant to tell Nancy about any of it. In 20 minutes on a Friday afternoon, though, with their son still sleeping peacefully in the next room, he does something he'd never really planned to do. He confesses.

Nancy doesn't cry, or scream, or throw hairbrushes. She listens calmly while her husband gives her a rough outline of what has replaced weight-lifting and sprinting in his life the past two months.

"Well," she says with a sigh when Sam stops, "you'd better keep packing. Don't want to miss that fishing trip."

Sam wants to ask her if he should pack for more than a weekend. Instead, he says, "I can't do that. I can't go away until we've talked this out."

Nancy shakes her head as if she's trying to clear it.

"I don't believe a weekend is going to make much difference," she says. "I think it might be better if we didn't try to clean up this mess until you get back."

Sam can't think of anything to say that won't make things

worse. Finally, he finishes packing and goes downstairs to get his fishing equipment.

Nancy hears Bobby Dance's truck as it turns into the driveway, throwing gravel on the patio bricks. She goes to the window to see Sam as he leaves. Bobby and Dave Faris are in the front, both with longneck beer bottles in their hands. Bobby blows the horn.

Nancy sees movement out of the corner of her eye and turns to see Sam, wearing the flannel L.L. Bean shirt she bought him for Christmas. His eyes are red.

"I do love you," he says hoarsely.

Nancy stares at him, a cool, neutral look, as he turns and heads down the stairs and out the door. It occurs to her that it's the first time Sam has said those words since they moved to Monacan, and she wonders if even the worst disasters don't have their up sides.

She'd considered, briefly, telling Sam about her fling with Buddy. She was halfway resolved to tell him about it anyhow, when she approached him just an hour before. Sam's guilt, which she mistook for pure lack of interest, had driven her to the point where she felt any change would be for the better.

But now, with something maybe worth saving after all, she knows that Sam might not forgive her for the very same thing of which he's been guilty. She thinks that she really does want to save their marriage, if she can resist cutting Sam's throat in a fit of jealousy when he sleeps. Well, she tells herself, I've got a weekend to figure out whether to change the locks or not.

She remembers something her mother told her after Suzanne found out she and Buddy were separated.

Suzanne had discovered her crying quietly in her and Pat's bedroom and soon ferreted out the truth, so she told her a story, one Nancy hadn't heard before. It happened when Nancy was six and the younger girls were 3 and 1, Suzanne said. She'd found out that Pat had slept with another woman, at least once while Suzanne was still in the hospital after giving birth to Candy. She told Nancy how Pat had cried and begged her forgiveness when he was confronted, and how loving he'd been afterward, almost a different person from the rough brawler she'd married.

When she finished telling the story, Nancy asked her how she could forgive her husband for cheating on her when she was in the hospital with a new-born baby.

"Honey," she told Nancy, putting her hand on her knee, "sometimes I think they all cheat. The only marriages that survive, it seems like to me, are the ones where the wife can take a joke."

She got up and handed her daughter a handkerchief from the bedside table.

"Besides," she said as she grabbed the doorknob, "Momma's had her times, too. But Daddy can't know about that. Men can't handle it." And she winked at Nancy as she slipped out the door.

Nancy is thinking of this when she hears Wade's first burbling, waking-up sounds.

Yes, she thinks to herself. I believe I can take a joke.

CHAPTER TWENTY-THREE

Wormwood. That's what I been tasting. In the dream, that fat lightning is turned into wormwood, just like in Revelation, where it says the third part of the waters becomes wormwood, and many men die.

Many men ought to die. All the cheating and whoring going on, it's a wonder God lets it go on.

Even Carter's boy. He thinks don't anybody know him and that yellow-haired woman is going out to that Holiday Inn, but I seen 'em. Seen his car there one morning when I was driving in to town, so I just parked my car in the back of the parking lot and waited. Sure enough, it won't 20 minutes before her and him come out, her first, pushing back her hair so she didn't look like they'd just been doing it. They'd parked their cars right next to each other, but they come out maybe 50 feet apart, like they was pulling something over on everybody.

But then, he walks over to her car and leans down and they kiss right there in broad-open daylight, all the cars and trucks going by right behind 'em on the interstate. I reckon Carter's boy's wife ain't no better than him, probably slipping around, too. They all do it. I read about it in them magazines like they sell in the stores in Richmond. Pure filth.

And they got the nerve to talk about me and Sebara. I can see folks turn away when I go get groceries, and then hear all that talking behind my back, like what they done when they started telling all them lies about me and Holly. Well, it's God's will, me and Sebara. It's His way to make His will known to all these sinful people. It's right funny, how nobody much from around here comes any more, just outsiders. Sebara says it's like when Jesus was turned on by his own people. She said it'd be folks from far off that would spread the word about Jesus-on-the-barn.

Feel right bad about the Jeter boy and all. But he was working for the devil. I seen that girl and him there that night, doing the devil's mischief right there on the ground in front of my barn, right where them pilgrims was standing not two hours before, worshipping. It had to be dealt with.

But they didn't see me. I made a noise so they'd hear, and I heard her run away, but I acted like I didn't see or hear nothing. I asked the Jeter boy if he'd help me the next afternoon moving some things, and he asked me how much I'd pay him. I told him $20 for three hours' work, which is more than I'd ever pay a sorry young'un like that to lift and tote.

The next day, he come up here 45 minutes late, shiftless just like all them Jeters. I made out like I had something I wanted to pull up out of the old irrigation pond, and that got him interested. Folks around here think I got treasure buried or something. Some even follows me when I go back in the woods; I never have caught 'em, but I can hear the leaves moving behind me when I'm being followed, which is more often than you'd think.

We walk down there to the pond, because it's so wet back there. He's got on tennis shoes, and he's cussing to beat the band because he's getting mud on 'em.

When we get to the pond, I take him right up to the edge and point towards a piece of a stick that's up out of the water, and I tell him that's where what I want pulled up is sunk, that there's a net under the water with something in it, and all he's got to do is hook the net. I hand him the rod and reel I'm carrying, tell him I'd do it myself, but I ain't so young anymore, don't think I can pull in anything that big. And he swallers it, hook, line and sinker. He's ready to pull him in some buried treasure, probably knock me over the head and run with it.

He never even seen that hickory stick I had set there next to the trail that morning. The first blow I hit him, I come down on him with both hands from behind, while he's thinking about getting rich quick, I reckon. He falls in the pond, but he tries to get back out, and I hit him again, right between the eyes, and he goes down for good. Little bubbles come up for a while, then nothing.

I throwed that stick in the middle of the pond and walked on back to the house. Next day, there come a thunderstorm and washed away all the footprints, just like I knowed it would. I kept on waiting for that boy's body to show up, for somebody to find him, but he must of got caught up in all the junk at the bottom of the pond. I couldn't even go down to my own pond 'til somebody finally found him.

When they did, the deputy come by one day and asked me some questions. "Did you know that boy?" "Did he hang around here much?" and such as that. I answered 'em and they never come back.

When I was a young'un, sometimes I'd get so mad about something that somebody did that Warren'd have to pull me off of him. This time, there weren't no Warren around.

Some might say it ain't right to punish like that, but I just think about Isaiah, how when the young'uns come up a'mocking him and all, he called a bear down out of the mountains, and it carried them young'uns away. Sometimes God's judgment is right harsh, but it is God's judgment, and somebody has got to be His instrument.

I didn't ask for none of this.

CHAPTER TWENTY-FOUR

When Sebara was just nine years old, she woke her mother and father on a cold, windy Thursday morning and told them she had dreamt of buried silver.

Lucas Tatum wasn't averse to listening to a child's dream. Ever since he fell off the roof, he had wanted badly to hear evidence of that voice again, the one that advised him to jump in his hour of need. He had some faith, but he wanted to know.

So Lucas and his wife, Annie, got up in the 6 o'clock darkness and listened as Sebara told them about her dream.

It was about something round, buried under the dirt at the edge of a field, she told them, right beside a crepe myrtle bush. Inside it was all kinds of silver. She told them that in her dream it was right underneath a big black rock.

Lucas grew quiet while Annie asked her daughter could she show them where it was. Sebara was silent for a moment, then said she thought she could. It was just Lucas and Annie and Sebara by this time living in the back of the old store.

"Maybe it was something that old man Cates buried before he died, and nobody would of knowed where it was," Annie said, and Lucas just nodded, somewhat sadly.

At dawn, the three of them went outside. Sebara rubbed her eyes. She and her mother both had on sweaters against the cold November wind; Lucas had on an old jacket with the zipper broken.

"Girl," he said to Sebara, limping along beside her, "you'd better not be messin' with me. It's a sin to claim gifts if they ain't no gifts."

She looked up at him, wide brown eyes showing hurt.

"I just know what I dreamt, Daddy," she said.

So she led her parents, as in a dream, out into the back yard, on past the pecan trees and the swing set nobody swung on anymore and the old Ford on blocks, to where the crepe myrtle sat, naked as a bundle of sticks, at the edge of Annie's collard patch.

Lucas could feel sweat under his jacket and shirt and undershirt. How could a child know? Jesus must of told her. Lucas knew, when he prayed and when he was in the throes of a sermon such as made little children wet their pants, that Jesus saw everything. But in the everyday world of bills and new school clothes, when he counted that offering and there was nobody to check after him, he sometimes felt like Jesus couldn't have his eyes on everything at the same time, that even Jesus must wink at a crippled black preacher trying to put food on the table by slipping a few quarters, even a dollar or two, out now and then.

Lucas hadn't spent a cent of it, he kept telling himself, just saving it for when something was needed. Why, it was just like old Joseph telling them Egyptians to save their grain for the lean years. Lucas had taken a liking to a somewhat used Chevrolet that Brother William Edes had for sale, which Brother Edes said he would sell for $150 down and $25 a month for the next two years, but nothing could make him dig up what he had come to think of as his insurance for something as carnal as a Chevrolet.

Sebara didn't start digging right away. She circled it with her eyes half-closed for a full two minutes before walking to the piece of coal Lucas put there to help him find the place.

"This is it," she said, firm with conviction.

Annie and she fell into digging. Lucas watched with his hands in his pockets. It took them all of 30 seconds to uncover the coffee can from the tilled earth at the edge of the garden, another 10 to pop open the lid.

"Lord Jesus," Annie said, looking up at Lucas. "The child done worked a miracle."

There was silver and green all over the bare ground. Annie and Sebara counted it right there: One hundred and fourteen dollars and fifty cents.

"Praise the Lord," Lucas said, thinking about the nights he'd gone out and dug that can up to add four or five dollars

151

to it. He'd been doing it all year, and he silently mouthed the amount along with Annie as she gave him a total he could have given her just as well. He was glad to know that Annie could count so well.

The word soon spread, by Annie, and Lucas was obliged to tell the congregation officially about it from the pulpit. From that day until his death 10 years later, he assumed that Jesus was watching him like a hawk.

What he never counted on was the deviousness of the nine-year-old mind. Sebara never missed a creak of the boards or a door lightly opened and then closed. She'd dug the can up herself once, when her parents were visiting at the rest home and she'd told them she had an upset stomach. She was just waiting for the right moment.

Sebara knew that she could have dug up the can herself and hid the money somewhere else, but she reasoned that there was no way a child could spend that kind of money and not draw attention to herself. Besides, she felt, in some way beneath and beyond thought, that she could better secure her future by being stamped as "special," than by covertly spending $114.50. When it came time to decide who would succeed Lucas Tatum as minister, there were few who didn't remember that God had spoken to Lucas' little girl.

Now, 20 years later, Sebara hasn't forgotten how to watch and listen.

She's been watching Lot Chastain out of the corner of her eye for two months now. She knows that he never goes to the bank, because the time they went in together to start the joint account, he acted as if he'd never been inside the building before in his life.

"Damn banks," he said to her after they'd left. "Like to of ruint Daddy and them in the Depression. Don't trust 'em."

Sebara knows that Lot cashes the Social Security check he gets once a month at his brother's store, and she knows that he's got some kind of trust from which he gets money, too. One time, when she asked him if he didn't have trouble paying the electricity and phone bills and taxes on such a big place, he gave her a quick sideways look and said, "My momma took care of that."

Two weeks before the last appearance of Jesus-on-the-barn, Sebara finally figures it out.

Other than some of his clothes and the television, the only thing Lot has taken from his trailer to his parents' house is his King James Bible.

One night, while Lot is in the bathroom down the hall, Sebara opens the Bible. There's a family tree in the front of it, and down in the right-hand corner of the first right-hand page, there's some scribbling. She finally makes out "Rev. 14:18." She turns to Revelation, the 14th chapter, 18th verse, and sees that part of the verse is underlined lightly in pencil: "Thrust in thy sharp sickle, and gather the clusters of the vine of the earth; for her grapes are fully ripe." In the margin between the verses was written in barely legible pencil: 14L,36R,7L.

The next time she goes for a midnight walk after Lot's fallen asleep, she doesn't visit Billy in the tent she's told him he can abandon for a place with her on the beach in Florida as soon as they make one last haul. Instead, she gets the flashlight out of her car and goes over to the northeast corner of the lot, out of sight of the big house, walking so lightly she barely disturbs the grass and clay.

The Chastains, like most farm families in Mosby County, raised every kind of fruit that could be canned or otherwise preserved for the winter. The apple and pear and peach trees are still there, eaten up by insects and still stubbornly bearing fruit every year. And right in the middle is the grapevine.

It's a rectangle six feet off the ground, set up on six poles. The vines were trained to grow around the horizontal boards on top, so that a person could pick grapes from a standing position. It hasn't been tended for years, but like the fruit trees, it still bears. Sebara can still smell the sweetness, even though summer's gone. She gropes around in the darkness of the new moon, and whatever she touches leaves her hands with a stickiness that she has nowhere to wash off.

Sebara knows that Lot has been here; she's seen his footprints before during an afternoon walk. Now, scouring the ground with the light, she thinks she knows why he comes here.

In the middle of the structure, where it seems another supporting pole should have been planted, she sees that the earth has been disturbed. She finds a stick and digs down into the earth with it. No more than six inches down, she meets resistance. Digging now with her hands, she touches metal and knows her suspicions were correct: Lot Chastain does not trust his money to banks.

"Praise Jesus," she murmurs and quickly pushes the dirt back over the top of the strongbox. She walks lightly back toward her car with her hands in front of her like a sleep-walker in the pitch black.

The last evening that the vision can be seen on Lot's barn is a Saturday in early October, the conclusion of a golden day fit for dove hunting and college football. Lot sits on the big house's front porch and listens to dogs running two farms away while Sebara is setting up the rental folding chairs for the final service. The smoke from the sawdust pile is blown away from the house by a favorable breeze.

They've had to move the chairs back almost to the edge of the woods in order to accommodate all the people they're expecting. Last night, almost 500 came, and they were generous. A group of black ministers from other churches in distant counties brought a gift of almost $2,000, mostly in worn bills of small denomination.

Lot and Sebara have deduced that the sun will set around 6:40. Sebara has started putting the time of sunset on their sign at the turnoff on Route 17, so that no one will miss anything.

Billy has been helping Sebara set everything up. While Lot sits on the front porch, she goes over their plans one last time.

"Soon as the old fool goes to sleep," she tells him, busily opening folding chairs and placing them in straight rows as she talks in a calm, quiet voice, "I'll get up and go. While I'm driving over to my place and emptying the safe there, you got to go dig up the strongbox where I showed you and empty it into the bag."

Billy nods as he dusts off the chairs' seats.

"Then I meet you out on the road, around the curve between here and Jeter's," he says, "and we'll be in Florida by morning. How much you reckon we got?"

"Well," Sebara says, "we must of got close to $6,000 last night, probably more tonight. I reckon, maybe $50,000, plus what all's in that strongbox."

Sebara knows exactly how much money Lot has hidden in the strongbox over the years, because she's tested the combination herself, on a second trip to the grapevine. But she isn't telling Billy that. Their pact is sealed, in his mind, because she wouldn't leave without the contents of the strongbox and he wants half of what's in the safe. Plus, he concludes, she's got a car that can get them to Florida, plus a cousin in South Carolina who can give them the license plates from a junked truck in his back yard.

"This time tomorrow," she tells Billy, never changing her expression, "you'll be drinking one of them pina coladas on the beach in Florida. Don't look like you just won the lottery, boy. He'll see you."

By 4 p.m., people are arriving. Some bring picnic suppers and blankets and go to the hayfields. Others just walk around the barn as if they are either trying to memorize it or seeking the answer to its riddle. A field mouse leaps from the leveled hay and children scream in surprise. Sebara has persuaded Lot to tie Granger's leash to the back of the house so that he doesn't scare the pilgrims, and his occasional bark can be heard above the crowd's murmur.

A reporter and photographer from the Times-Dispatch are there, and half the others present seem to have cameras with them. The whiskey barrel has been replaced by several smaller containers so that none of the pilgrims is more than 20 feet away from one.

Sebara is more the show now than the image of Jesus on the cross. She realizes that she and Lot might have overextended themselves by one day, that perhaps Friday was the last day you could really see the image at all. Only a person with a strong imagination can really make out anything from the lines in the faded old building. For a minute, maybe two, just as the sun disappears at its more and more oblique angle, a golden ray hits the building in just the right way and several people say, almost in unison, "I see it! I see it!"

155

"The LOOOORD giveth," intones Sebara, so loudly that several people jump and a baby starts crying, "and the LOOORD taketh away. BLESSED is the name of the Lord." A few "Amens" are heard through the packed crowd bundled against the fast-approaching evening chill.

Sebara, half singing and half preaching, tells the crowd that there must be a shrine to Jesus in order for Him to come back next spring. She tells them that they need $10,000 more to start building on that shrine, that they'll build all winter, even in the snow, to have it ready by next April, to show their faith and love for their saviour.

By 7:15, she's finished. She leads them in singing "Amazing Grace," and the faithful reach for their pocketbooks and wallets. A man from Michigan gives Sebara 10 $100 bills and says that he's never really believed in God until he saw that one glimpse of the vision. He's driven all night to get to Monacan for the last service of the year, slept in his car in the courthouse parking lot, and now he's going to drive back.

"Praise Jesus," she says to the man, who's badly in need of a shave and is crying. She puts her hands on both sides of his head like a faith-healer and says, "You have a safe trip back, now."

The deputy sheriff in charge of traffic has been joined by two others, but even with some of the people straggling to get one last look at Lot's barn, there's a 90-minute traffic jam out to the state highway. By the time Lot and Sebara have collected the money from the boxes and can go inside to dinner, it's after 9 o'clock.

Lot lets Billy have dinner with them. Sebara has gone out earlier in the day for barbecue, and now all she has to do is warm it and the hushpuppies and break out the coleslaw.

Billy is starving. He hasn't eaten since breakfast and is running out of money. He's happy that he and Sebara finally have what they need. But he knows better than to start eating until after Lot asks the blessing. While the old man is praying, he looks up through squinted eyes and sees Sebara looking at him. She winks and he smiles.

Sebara is sitting in the driver's seat of her Lincoln, watching the last moths of the season flitter around the outside porch light of her cousin's cinder-block house. It's 4:30, still a good three hours until dawn. The South Carolina air feels warm and damp to her, like the sea, and she feels as if the ocean itself must be just beyond the stand of pines that a full moon highlights in the distance behind the house.

Her cousin, a gap-toothed man much darker than Sebara, is busy changing the plates on the car. His wife and family are asleep inside; Sebara told him when she called that she'd just as soon make it short and sweet. Save the visit for another time.

Ten minutes and he's done. He comes around to the driver's side.

"You bury them plates, now," she tells him as she hands him five 20-dollar bills. He nods and asks her again doesn't she want a bite to eat.

"Gotta go," she says, cranking the car carefully so as not to wake up any more of the dogs along the dirt street.

By 11:30, half an hour after Lot took the pills that Sebara had been giving him for the last month to help him sleep, he had stopped moving. She waited for another 30 minutes, though. When the clock chimed midnight, she slipped out of the old feather bed, the one thing on the Chastain property that she hated to leave behind, and got dressed quickly, not even bothering with underwear.

She almost screamed when she ran into Billy Basset as she tiptoed down the front steps. He was supposed to wait for her to blink the car lights as a signal to start digging underneath the grapevine.

"Peckerhead!" she hissed at him, then calmed herself. "You was supposed to wait for me over by the tent."

"Was afraid you won't coming," he said.

"I'm here," she said, "and I'll be here again in 45 minutes. You better have that strongbox money. All of it. You got the bag?"

Billy nodded, holding up the deposit bag, and walked off toward the grapevine. Sebara watched him go for perhaps 10 seconds, then headed for the car.

She backed out the driveway and was around the bend from the Chastain house before she turned on the lights. She was on Route 17, headed south, before she allowed herself the luxury of pulling off at an abandoned gas station to look in the trunk one more time.

She turned the key and the mammoth Lincoln trunk sprung open to reveal two gym bags. She couldn't quite get all the bills from the pilgrims' donations in the first one, so she had to commingle some of them with the cash she had removed from Lot's strongbox the night before.

She figured that, by now, Billy Basset would be getting ready to work the combination on the old box, and that in a minute or two he would discover that it was empty.

Sebara had gone out earlier in the day to her home to withdraw the cash from her safe, then added their take from the last night to it, telling Lot that the money would be more secure if she put it in the car trunk until Monday morning when she could deposit it.

"Unless you got a safe or something around here we can put it in," she'd said, looking into his eyes.

He'd shaken his head wordlessly, looking away.

Sebara rolls the glass up as she approaches the paved road that leads back to I-95 and pops a Marvin Gaye tape into the tape deck. She's still clear-eyed, not sleepy a bit, thanks to the speed she usually only takes before preaching a sermon.

She can almost feel herself vibrating to the background of "I Heard It Through the Grapevine," which always reminds her of jungle drums.

She thinks about the grapevine back behind Lot Chastain's house and bursts into uncontrollable laughter. She's still laughing when she reaches the interstate and takes the south exit, toward Florida.

CHAPTER TWENTY-FIVE

*E*verybody's all the time trying to take me for a fool. Carter and Aileen and them just aching to sell this land right out from under me. Them folks from the historical society wanting me to give it to 'em, like I owed them something. The sheriff and the fire chief threatening me because I won't let them put out the sawdust pile.

And now Sebara. Took me a spell to figure out what was making me so groggy of a morning. Couldn't wake up, and then I was ready to take a nap by the middle of the afternoon. That ain't like me.

Finally, I seen it was them pills, the ones that's supposed to make me sleep. Like I need to sleep. Didn't swaller the one night before last, or last night, just to see what happened. I played like I was sleeping, though.

Tonight, I seen what their game was. Can't fool Lot Chastain forever.

Wasn't half a hour after I started playing possum when I heard the bed creak and her slip out of it quiet as a mouse, old boards creaking with every tip-toe. I got good ears for a old man. Heard her open the closet and take something out. Heard her all the way down the hall. Heard the front door open soft as moonlight. Even heard feet walking in the front yard and whispers, like it was two people instead of just the one.

Playing possum. Like when I was a young'un. Warren was oldest, then me a year later, and then Carter and Aileen. And then Grace and finally Holly. There'd be two sleeping in there with Momma and Daddy, the baby and the knee-baby, so it was Aileen that moved me out. I wasn't but five.

I didn't want to stay in that big old room down the hall. Warren'd had to sleep down there by himself for a year already, since Carter come, but I didn't want no part of it. Some nights, I'd slip back in Momma and Daddy's room. If Daddy was awake, he'd make me go

159

back to my room, said he'd beat me good if I didn't go. But if I waited, he'd fall asleep and Momma would still be awake, and she'd let me crawl in there, my knees up against her back, spoon-like, and she'd wake up before Daddy in the morning and send me back to my room. If Daddy woke up first, he'd make me go on back down the hall. I was seven when I stopped.

Last time I stayed with Momma and Daddy, I woke up and thought I was in my own room, because there wasn't any body next to mine. And then I heard the noises, and for the first time I reckon I had a notion what the noises was. When I looked over at them, Momma was under Daddy and she looked at me, and the look was like "Don't let on you're awake" and "I'm sorry. I can't help it."

I didn't come back no more after that.

But I got right good at playing possum over the years. You could find out all kinds of things about folks by playing possum. Like Sebara.

I go into the front room, real quiet, and I can see them in the full moon outside. I stay back in the shadows and watch her when she goes towards her car and he walks off in the other direction.

I don't open that door until I hear the car start, and then I follow the boy. Figure she'll be coming back for him.

The steps feel cold under my feet, but I don't have no time to get no slippers. I can still hear her car off in the distance, and I can just barely see something, maybe the flash of a watch in the moonlight, off to my right.

Seems like the Lord is always giving me some sign. I meant to put that hoe up after I weeded last time, but there it still sat, right by the front steps, saying, "Use me."

The boy's trail isn't hard to follow. Partly I can see the footprints, partly I can hear him, on up ahead there, down on his knees like he might be praying. He's on all fours like some animal, breathing hard and making some digging sound.

The moon looks red, like it does when the wind blows the smoke right, and the smell of sawdust is stinging my nose, making me think about fat lightning for some reason. It isn't much above 40 degrees, but it don't seem to hit me except for my feet, not 'til afterwards.

Sometimes at night, I can see something better by not looking right at it, like there's a blind spot right ahead. I can see the boy up ahead a ways, but it's like you see something out of the corner of your eye.

I can't focus on him, but it don't take me too long to figure out where he is and what he's up to.

I slip around to the back of him, not making hardly a sound when I tip-toe past the apple trees, up by the pear tree. It's so bright that I can see my shadow cast all the way to the edge of the field, but that boy, he ain't looking nowhere but down.

Ten feet behind him and he still hasn't heard nothing. He's breathing hard, and I think for a minute how he smoked them cigarettes all the time, and how if he had of been in better shape, he might of not been so out of breath and might of heard me.

He's dug it up, I can see that. And he's opened it. One of 'em must of got the combination, or picked the lock. I can hear him cussing, the bad words coming out every time he catches his breath. "God damn black whore. Fucking cunt." Just terrible language. And he's a-crying. I near-bout felt sorry for him, because it's right clear to me already that she's fooled us both. But then I think about what all was in that box, and what's not in it now.

Daddy said not never to trust banks.

He said he'd of been a rich man now if he'd of just dug him a hole in the back yard and buried all he saved in the '20s. When Monacan Trust closed the doors in 1932, it like to of wiped Momma and Daddy out. And Daddy would always point out the bank president to me when I was with him in town, how he didn't look like he'd lost a thing, just kept on wearing them fine suits and driving a new car.

Hell, Daddy said, he probably buried his money in a sock in the back yard. He had more sense than to put it in any damn bank.

After the bank lost all Daddy's money, they had the nerve to repossess his John Deere 'cause he couldn't keep up the payments. We plowed with a mule for six years after that.

I let Sebara talk me into putting the Jesus money in an account, but it didn't set right with me. She told me it was OK, that we'd just be putting it there for a little spell 'til we got enough to break ground on the shrine we was going to build.

Should of put it right out here under the grapevine with all the rest of it. But now that's gone, too.

If Daddy got a little money for his tobacco or his beans or for clearing some land, he'd give Momma some and he'd bury the rest, right out here by the grapevine. He dug up some for Holly's wedding,

and he give some to Carter and Aileen and Grace for their young'uns'
education, not that any of 'em appreciated it. I reckon a lot of folks
took to keeping what money they could save in jars and socks and
such after the Depression hit, but Daddy didn't never stop doing it,
not 'til he died in 1946.

The day after we buried him, Momma had me take a shovel and
dig up the strong box. We counted near-bout $25,000, some of it in
tens and twenties, some of it in silver dollars. Momma told me to
take the silver dollars.

"You got it coming to you," she said. "He didn't dig up none of it
for you."

There was 87 of 'em. I never did spend them, just give some away.

When we went through the plunder room after Momma died, we
found hundreds of dollars that she must of hid in mattresses and
such up there. It was like a damn Easter egg hunt, me and Carter
and the girls trying to see who could find the most.

But I been putting money into that old strong box for 25 years
since Daddy died, and, Lord, there must of been $50,000 in there
if there was a cent.

Oh Lord! There's always somebody coming around to mess things
up! I didn't want none of this. All I wanted was for to be left alone.
I didn't ask for no vision on my barn, and I sure didn't ask for
anybody to steal everything I ever saved, leaving me here looking
like a fool.

The hoe shakes in my hand, not 'cause I'm scared, but because
I'm fighting the urge to start smashing down on that boy's skull right
now. But I got to get closer. Little closer . . .

I can't get the hoe much higher than my head, can't bring it all
the way back like I want to, because of the grapevine up above me.
But the first lick hits him clean in the back of his head. It seems like
he must of heard the hoe whistling through the cold night air, because
he made just a twitch before it hit him. The hoe sinks in a little bit,
and I have to yank hard to pull it out, like when you hit a green
piece of wood with the axe and it just closes in around the blade. He
screams a little, like a pig at hog-killing, and he rolls over.

I keep on hitting him, and you can't hardly tell he's got a face no
more after a while. I reckon I must of kind of blanked out, and this
goes on for what must of been a right good while, because when

I stop, my arms ache from bringing it down so many times. So many times.

I look at the hoe handle, and there's yellow hairs all caught up in it, stuck with all the blood. The boy, you don't want to look at him. There's part of a hand that don't even touch anything else, and the ground is soaked.

I go back to the house and turn on the outside faucet. I wash all the blood and hair off the hoe. Then I put it back where I picked it up.

CHAPTER TWENTY-SIX

The strange thing to Nancy, now that Marilou and Buddy are dating, is that he and Pat act as if they can't get enough of each other. They go to Richmond Braves baseball games, have a beer afterward at Chiocca's and seem like long-lost friends united at last. It's hard for Nancy to believe that Pat withheld money for her college education because she married Buddy out of high school.

She mentions this to Pat in a quiet moment when Suzanne is clearing the dishes and father and daughter are sitting on chaise lounges on the back porch, Wade leaning contentedly against his grandfather.

"Well," Pat says, cutting his eyes toward his daughter as he takes the Miller tall-neck from his lips, "he's grown up a lot. He's not the same shithead used to take you parking out by the airport.

"Besides," he says, as a prelude to taking another sip, "you were the oldest."

The silence in the O'Neils' back yard is broken only by the sound of televisions leaking through look-alike brick ranchers up and down the street. It is a pleasant squawk to Nancy, reminiscent of her loud, happy childhood here, promising a Monopoly game soon with both parents and all children old enough to roll the dice eligible to play.

The last sunlight is hitting high in the oaks, which always turn more quickly in the city, Nancy has noticed. It's sweater weather, and they'll have to go in soon, but she feels more relaxed than she has in days. She makes a note to get a chaise lounge for their back porch in Monacan. Assuming, she quickly corrects herself, that she will have a back porch in Monacan much longer.

164

She was out on the highway, headed for Richmond, half an hour after Sam left. Nancy tries to plan her "home visits" on nights and weekends when Sam's gone, as much as possible. Her family wants to like Sam, she honestly believes, but his silences just make them louder and more outrageous than usual. Quiet is not something with which the O'Neils are comfortable.

Nobody asks about Sam, but nobody asks about Buddy either, despite the fact that Suzanne and Pat obviously know something's not quite right. Nancy appreciates the rare deference shown by her parents, whose invasions of her privacy kept her blushing for most of her adolescent years. She almost envied friends who complained that their parents never told them anything about sex. Suzanne and Pat were shameless, laughing uproariously at each other's dirty jokes and inviting their children to do the same.

"Nancy, honey," Suzanne told her when she was only 13, just introduced to spin-the-bottle at birthday parties, "boys can be real nice, but you've got to remember: A stiff dick has no conscience."

She and Marilou used to howl in their shared double bed at night over the directness of Suzanne's and Pat's advice. Nancy gives an involuntary snort of a laugh now, remembering her mother's earnest look on that long-ago day.

Pat gives a start.

"Almost time for the game," he says.

It's the night of the third game of the World Series. Suzanne tells Nancy that Candy is bringing a boyfriend, and Robbie said he and his date might stop by later.

"You know," Nancy says to her mother, who's popping popcorn, "you can invite Marilou and Buddy. It doesn't matter."

"Hell," Suzanne says, "I did invite them. Marilou said they might come over later, just to watch you throw up in the rose bushes."

Nothing, Nancy thinks to herself, is sacred around here.

Eventually, 15 people are squeezed into the O'Neils' 15x14 living room. Nancy puts Wade to bed in the third inning, and she squeezes into an opening along the floor, between Robbie and Candy's date. She wonders, not for the first time, why some people's houses seem to have neon welcome signs out front. There were plenty of living rooms, plenty of houses, larger than her parents' when she was growing up, but anyone in the neighborhood missing a kid always checked at the O'Neils' place first.

Marilou and Buddy do make it, and Nancy and Buddy nod in passing a couple of times. During the seventh-inning stretch, they run into each other in the hallway leading to the guest bathroom.

"Have you forgiven me?" he asks her.

"Nothing to forgive you for."

"Can we be friends, even if I marry Marilou?"

"It depends on what you call friends," Nancy says.

Buddy backs away a step, palms upraised. "No. No. I mean, friends-friends. I just don't want you to hate me."

Nancy gives him a hug. "Not frigging likely," she says.

"You and Sam getting along?" he asks her.

"Yeah. Great," she lies, "as long as he doesn't find out about you. Why do you ask?"

Buddy puts his hands in his pockets and leans against the wall.

"Well," he says, "I don't think what happened would have happened if everything was great."

"It's OK," she tells him. "I think it's going to be OK."

Saturday, Nancy and Suzanne go shopping and then to a movie. They and Pat and Robbie and his date go to a Chinese restaurant for dinner Saturday night. Nancy's fortune reads: "Love will return and grow." She hopes it's an optimistic sign. Pat tells a joke about a great Dane with long toenails.

She leaves Richmond at 2 Sunday afternoon because she's promised Sam's parents that she and Wade will come by. Marie's brother from Ohio, an old widower who has never seen either of them, is in town.

Nancy thought she had become accustomed to the silences of Sam's family. After a weekend with Pat and Suzanne, though, the ticking of the clock between terse sentences weighs on her. She gets up every 10 minutes to check on Wade, playing in the back yard with toys his grandparents have bought just for his visits.

"Do you remember Ansel Wagram?" Marie asks her brother.

He looks puzzled. Finally, he says, "I was in school with a Wagram."

"That's the one," Marie says.

Silence.

Finally, "Well, I guess I don't remember him too well."

"He died."

Silence.

Nancy finds herself blending into her environment.

When she first met Sam's parents, Carter or Marie would ask her a question about her family, and she would launch into a five-minute story about something insane that Suzanne or Pat or one of her siblings had done. She soon realized, though, that the Chastains weren't so much listening politely to her as sitting open-mouthed at such an eruption of words. She wondered if they weren't turning to each other, the moment the front door closed behind their son and his date, and shaking their heads in unison.

They don't even seem to be able to work up a good head of steam about Lot and Jesus-on-the-barn. Like the rest of the Chastains, Carter and Marie seem embarrassed by the circus-like atmosphere the vision has created at Old Monacan. Last night was the final service until the sundown light will hit the back of the structure again in the spring, and Carter says he heard that there were several hundred people there, cars backed all the way to the state highway.

"Good riddance," Marie sniffs.

"I knew a man once," says her brother from Ohio, "that said he saw the image of Christ on the wall of the men's room at his service station. Couldn't nobody else see it, though."

"Said they raised almost $10,000 last night," Carter offers.

Marie shakes her head.

Silence.

Nancy endures it until half past five. Then, 30 seconds into another chasm of unbroken silence, she stands abruptly.

"I guess we'd better be running along," she says.

"Take the car; it'll be quicker," says Carter. He winks at her.

Nancy tells them that she wants to go out to Old Monacan

for a few minutes. They know that she likes to write, although they don't quite understand why, and they know that whatever she is writing has something to do with Lot and the barn, so no one thinks this is an unusual thing to do, given who is doing it. She asks them if they'll look after Wade for a while.

She soothes her son, who screams and wails his desire to go with her. Nancy is tempted to take him, just for the comfort of having someone, even a 2-year-old, to talk to on the darkening road to Lot's barn. But she plans for this to be a short visit. She needs to see the old barn one more time, without all the pilgrims there and, she hopes, without Lot or Sebara or the Basset boy there either. The story she's writing has been on her mind over the weekend, a mental barrier, she supposes, to keep her from thinking about Sam any more than necessary, and she wants to just sit there, undisturbed, staring at the back of Lot's barn as the sun sets. The protagonist of her novel does just this as the book ends, and Nancy wants to feel what her creation feels.

Nancy is on the second step from the bottom, heading for the car, when she hears Marie calling her.

"Wait up, Nancy. Let me give you something for Lot. We had a plenty of roast beef left over."

Nancy curses under her breath. The last thing she wants to do, if she can help it, is have one of those awkward meetings with Sam's uncle. He reminds her of the old television show she used to watch on re-runs, where Groucho Marx would interview and humiliate people from Nebraska or Texas or wherever. If one of the guests said the magic word, a duck would come down from the ceiling and the guest would win a prize. With Lot, Nancy feels that the duck is never very far away. And she never knows what the magic word might be.

"Well," she tells Marie, "I'm not going to be long."

"Oh, that's OK," her mother-in-law says. "Just leave it with him. Lord, I don't know what all he eats out there. Don't even know if that colored woman cooks."

So Nancy carries a paper plate wrapped in tinfoil to the car, with a quarter of a pound cake wrapped in Saran Wrap and a plastic container full of potato salad balanced on top. Her purse is thrown over her shoulder.

"Sure you don't have a watermelon I can take in my free hand?" she mutters to herself as she opens the car door, furious that she has to perform this odious task, furious that she doesn't have the guts to just tell her in-laws she doesn't want to see Lot if at all possible.

It's 6:15 by the time she leaves the driveway. She can see that Wade is already being jollied out of his tantrum by his grandfather.

The sun will set in another 15 minutes, so she hurries through town and out to the state highway, then makes as much time as she can on the tight, shoulderless road to Lot's barn. When she passes the Jeter place, she sees that Simon Jeter has finally given up and let the road to Old Monacan take a detour through his bean field. He fought it for months, putting up barricades and digging trenches, but in the last week, with hundreds of cars a night coming through, Simon finally feared for his garage and was just happy to have the hordes of pilgrims pass as far away from his home as possible.

Nancy sees that the mourning wreath for Simon's grandson is still hanging on the door of the trailer nearest the road.

The sun is dead in Nancy's eyes now, coming in for a landing. She almost hits a stray dog who appears merely as a black shadow and then vanishes. This time of day, the naked clay where trees have been cleared turns a red that is painful to the eye. Nancy can feel her body unclench when she finally passes into the row of cedars that marks the beginning of the woods.

Here, night has already fallen, although the sky is blue overhead. Nancy fears she's too late, but when she turns the corner and comes up the slight rise, she can see the sun still hitting Lot's trailer.

She stops in front, where her car can't be seen from the house, closes the door softly and walks across to the barn, hoping for some peace before she has to confront Lot with his supper.

The area around the barn has the look of a fairgrounds the day after the carnival leaves town. The hard clay soil has been turned into mud by thousands of feet, and the smell is not unlike that of a hog pen. The trash from last night hasn't been cleaned up; even the metal chairs are as they were left by the final assault of pilgrims.

Nancy sits in one of the chairs nearest the edge of the viewing area and sees the sun hit the barn just above where the outline of the crucifixion could be seen a week ago. She squints, still seeing spots from the sun, but she realizes that Lot and Sebara must have squeezed the very last ounce of sunlight out of the vision. Jesus-on-the-barn won't be back until spring.

She sighs, sitting there in the hard metal chair, trying to imagine what her protagonist would have thought. The first evening wind blows the smell of cinders to her from the sawdust pile, and she shivers, feeling that she's being watched.

Nancy stays there for 10 minutes, and then she thinks she has what she needs. She turns toward her car, realizing that she has one more errand to do before she goes back to Monacan. She looks up toward the old house, now sinking into darkness, and realizes that every light in it must be on.

At least, she thinks, Sebara is around. Otherwise, I wouldn't be doing this.

She decides to drive up to the front of the house, rather than walk the 50 yards and then have to walk back again in the dark. After she's negotiated the old driveway and taken the cold supper out, she looks back eastward and sees the moon, one night past full, rising above the woods.

She walks up the front steps, balancing her load, and knocks on the front door. Invisible in the darkness beyond the side of the house, she can hear Granger pleading to be released from his chain so he can eat this intruder.

After knocking twice, Nancy turns the knob and the front door opens. The room into which she walks is the big living room where the family meets at Christmas and Easter. It smells of ammonia and cleanser, but the general appearance of the room is of chaos. Shirts and dresses thrown over the floor and across chairs. A sidetable overturned. A lamp broken.

She takes no more than six steps inside when she decides to go no farther. She bends slightly at the waist and sets the dinner from Marie down on top of the television set. Let him find it himself. Whatever's happened here, let it happen without me.

She turns to tip-toe out, just as the door opens.

"Well, hey there, Holly," Lot says, and Nancy feels a week's worth of adrenaline flash through her. His eyes are red and sunk deeper into his skull than usual.

"No. It's Nancy, Uncle Lot," she says. "Sam's wife."

"Don't you 'Uncle Lot' me," he says, more jolly than she's seen him in months. "Why don't you come see me more often, Holly?"

Nancy stands there, afraid to do anything. Lot's face changes in seconds.

"They cheated me, Holly," he says, and Nancy can see that his lips are trembling. "They cheated me. But I got even with 'em. They're always messing with me."

"Where's Sebara?" Nancy asks. She starts moving to the right, thinking that if she can get Lot to move a little farther into the room, she can run around the big livingroom couch and beat him to the door.

Lot looks puzzled.

"Who? Don't know no Sebara. Don't you be messin' with me too, Holly."

Nancy remembers now that she didn't see the big Lincoln out front when she drove up to the trailer, and she didn't see it outside the big house.

"I have to go now, Uncle Lot," she tells him, moving another step to the right, almost even with the other end of the couch now, as he moves a step forward.

"Why you call me that?" he asks her in a querulous voice. "Why is everybody a-trying to mess with my head?"

Nancy makes her move, pushing off from the couch and running for the front door. What does her in is the thumb bolt. Lot always locks it from the inside, and by the time Nancy figures out the workings of it, Lot has grabbed her right wrist.

"Please," she says, trying not to let him see how scared she is.

"Come on, Holly," Lot says, giving her a pull. "I want you to see what they done to me."

She can't believe how strong he is. He's pulling her along with one hand, and she has to run to keep up. She screams once, and he puts a big, freckled hand over her mouth and nose and tells her, "Now, you got to behave, Holly, or I won't take you to Egypt."

He takes her outside, to the other side of the house from the barn, toward the fruit trees where she was showing Wade the ready-for-picking apples a month ago. The moon is bright enough for Nancy to see them rotting on the ground as they go past. She sees that the yellow jackets have ruined them already.

They are almost to the grapevine when she sees the lump there, seemingly no larger than a dog.

"They took Daddy and Momma's money," Lot says, but all Nancy can see is what obviously was human a short while ago. She tries to step backward, but Lot won't let go.

"Won't be taking no more, though," he says, and then he turns Nancy a quarter-turn, facing him.

"Now, then. You see how he ought to of been killed, don't you?" Nancy nods. The moon shines off Lot's eyes, which look to be all black now. "It was like when they told all them lies about us. Some people, they don't deserve to live."

Nancy is crying.

"Don't you worry none, Holly," Lot says. "I know just what'll fix you up. We'll go over to Egypt. Wouldn't that be nice?"

Nancy has the feeling that she's in a dream, that surely she'll wake up in bed next to Sam's snoring. But it goes on. Lot drags her back from where they came, but when they get to the house, he doesn't take her back inside. Instead, they go past the barn. Nancy has stopped protesting that she isn't Holly, because that only makes Lot angrier.

Up ahead, there's only the sawdust pile. The smoke that rises from it day and night has turned the moon behind it a coppery-red.

"Now, first, before we go to Egypt," Lot tells Nancy, leaning so close to her ear that she can feel and smell his old-man's breath, "we got to tempt the devil."

Lot turns Nancy loose, then waits expectantly. She doesn't know what to do. For the first time in 20 minutes, her right wrist is free, but where to run?

Then, she remembers the game Carter told her about once, the game that Lot made the younger children play. Tempt the Devil. Run over the top of the sawdust pile to the other side. Maybe, she thinks, if I can get a running start, I can hide out in the woods, or double back to the road. She remembers how Sam always warned about staying away from the burning hill, because of cave-ins, but she also remembers what the remainder of Billy Basset's face looked like.

"Me first," she says, running away from Lot and up the side of the pile. The cinders immediately get into her loafers and cut like sandspurs, slowing her even more than the up-hill grade.

She stops less than halfway up, to catch her breath and try to empty the cinders from her shoes, when she hears the breathing behind her. Lot is following her up the hill.

She loses one shoe, turns and continues toward the top. Every time she tries to cut left or right, Lot does the same behind her, herding her toward the very top of the man-made hill.

"Egypt, Holly. Egypt next," she can hear him wheezing behind her. The smoke causes her eyes to tear and her nose to burn. She can hardly bear to put any weight on her feet now, and she finally loses the other shoe as she nears the top.

The pile gives worse than sand at the beach, but she finally crests the orange hill, with Lot only a few steps behind.

She's only just started down the other side of the pile when she loses her balance and topples forward, rolling, rolling forever, finally hitting the bottom, sawdust cinders stinging every part of her body.

Then she hears Lot. She looks up, squinting out of one eye, and he's silhouetted against the moon, at the pinnacle of the sawdust pile.

The last word she hears him say is "Egypt," and then there's a whistling noise. Lot seems to be shrinking before her, first slowly and then suddenly. The muffled sound of a five-story sawdust pile collapsing on itself is all she hears, then there's nothing. Sawdust cinders rain down all over and around her, and the smoke is almost blinding. She crawls away from the pile, feeling her way until she can breathe again.

The first thing she sees, when one eye has rid itself of the cinders enough to open it, is Lot's barn. She has wandered around the pile counter-clockwise toward the house. Ahead, she can see her car, and a quick check shows her that she hasn't lost the keys. The car starts on the second try, and Nancy hits the headlights.

In the distance, where the sawdust pile used to dominate the skyline, she can make out an almost-flat surface through the smoke and burning cinders, with a red moon behind it.

Carter answers the door. Nancy has already been by her house to brush the cinders out of her hair and clothes as best she can and put tennis shoes over her wounded feet. If Carter notices the change in clothes, he doesn't say anything.

"I think you'd better have somebody go out and check on Uncle Lot," she tells Carter. "I took his dinner inside, but he wasn't there, and something's happened to the sawdust pile."

Sam gets back home at 10:30. Coming around the last turn, he can make out lights in his and Nancy's house, and he knows she hasn't left him yet.

Bobby Dance and David Faris help him unload the cooler full of blues that somebody has to clean or give away, and then they're off into the night.

Sam hasn't had much sleep. Every time he would nod off, he'd think about Nancy and he'd wish he were back in Monacan. He made a long-distance call from Nags Head to tell Corinne that he couldn't see her anymore, and she took it more casually than his ego might have wished.

"Oh, that," she said. "Yeah, I think that might be a good idea, too." And she hung up on him.

Now, putting his tackle into the garage, he decides the fish have enough ice to last until morning, and he unlocks the front door. There's only the one light in the foyer downstairs. Upstairs, he can make out a glow somewhere, and he guesses Nancy is reading in bed.

Time, he guesses, to get the verdict.

He hears the drawers opening and closing, and as he nears the bedroom door, he sees the two suitcases Nancy is rapidly filling.

She's wearing an old sweatshirt and jeans. She has a Band-Aid over her left eyebrow, and she's limping for some reason.

She gives almost no indication that she's seen him until he moves toward her.

"The last bus for Richmond leaves in 10 minutes," she tells him, not bothering to look around. "If you're coming with me, you better start packing."

NOW

CHAPTER TWENTY-SEVEN

Suzanne and Marilou and the girls wait around until Nancy has signed a dozen or so copies of the book. Then it's their turn.

"Honey," Suzanne says, "I just wish Pat could've seen this. He would've been so proud."

Marilou just gives her sister the fish-eye and says, "EYE-ther?"

The girls, Nancy knows, would probably just as soon be somewhere else. Kate, who's 17 and favors Suzanne, gave up a Sunday afternoon date for this, and Polly, who's 14 and looks like her father, could have gone to Kings Dominion with her friends.

"Thanks for coming," Nancy tells them both. Kate shrugs; Polly gives her mother a kiss on the cheek.

"I never thought anybody'd ask me for my autograph," Nancy says.

"What'd you write?" Marilou asks. "Is it like yearbooks: 'To a really great girl. Best wishes'?"

"We need some men around here," Suzanne says, too loud, and a couple of matrons glance at her on the way out.

"Well," Nancy says, "you can't expect Wade to pass up a job interview. There'll be more of these. I'll get even, though. I won't go to his graduation."

"What time does your old man get back from that conference?" Suzanne asks.

"His plane got in about 45 minutes ago," Nancy says, looking at her watch. "I told him I'd meet him at home. You all're coming over, aren't you? We've got some celebrating to do."

Just then, the front door to the women's club swings open and a man with graying hair and a hurried, disheveled look walks in.

"Did I miss it?" he asks, looking from one woman to the other.

"Daddy!" Polly says. "Mom was great."

"You missed it," Nancy says, smiling, "but thanks for trying, sweetie."

And then Buddy Molloy gives his wife a big kiss, in front of everybody.

Sam never did come back. Nancy stayed at her parents' house for two days before he called, but by then everything was in such disarray, he said, that he felt he ought to stay for a while, to help deal with the police and reporters and gawkers.

So Nancy stayed with her parents. Two weeks turned into a month, with Sam coming to visit on weekends. He understood, he said, why Nancy would be shaken by all that had happened, although she never told him or anyone else more than she told the police: that she left dinner on the table in the Chastain house and never saw a living soul, just the collapsed sawdust pile. He wished that she would come back, but he didn't think he could leave Monacan for a while.

Five weeks after she moved back to Richmond, Buddy came by one Tuesday afternoon. Marilou and he were still dating, once a week or so, but Marilou wouldn't be home from work for three hours. Only Nancy and Suzanne were there, watching an old movie on TV.

Buddy asked Suzanne if he could talk with Nancy alone, and before she could answer, he took Nancy's hand and led her to the big den, Pat's room, in the back of the house.

And that's where Buddy Molloy proposed to Nancy for the second time.

She thought he was crazy at first, but he kept her in Pat's den for an hour and a half, and when they were through, she said she'd think about it. She couldn't believe she even said that. She was, as she pointed out half a dozen times, a married woman. He was, she pointed out a dozen times, dating her sister.

But Buddy Molloy felt that he had one last chance, and he wasn't going to mess it up. He stopped seeing Marilou and started "courting" Nancy. Suzanne and Pat didn't like it much when roses starting arriving, and they insisted that Nancy definitely would not be dating a man, even her former husband, while she and Sam weren't even separated. But they liked Buddy, and they did let him come over to visit, and they would let Nancy and him have the den to themselves occasionally.

On a January day, with snow covering the O'Neils' back yard, Nancy accepted Buddy's wedding proposal for the second time.

It was all very civil. As Nancy suspected, Sam couldn't work up enough enthusiasm to either try to woo her back or get very angry about his wife getting engaged while she was still married. They eventually decided that Wade would spend weeks with Nancy, weekends with Sam. Nancy went to Sam's father's and mother's funerals and stayed in touch with his aunts, who all died within a year of each other.

And Sam, five years after the divorce, married a 22-year-old redhead who, everyone in Monacan said, looked an awful lot like the former Corinne Cobb.

Marilou pitched a fit about the whole affair, from the time Buddy told her he intended to marry her sister again, and it would be two years later, at Marilou's wedding, before they made peace.

But within a year of the night that the sawdust pile collapsed and killed Lot Chastain, Nancy and Buddy were married. Candy and Robbie liked to refer to her as Nancy O'Neil Molloy Chastain Molloy.

She was relieved that her family had a sense of humor.

FRANKLIN COUNTY LIBRARY
906 NORTH MAIN STREET
LOUISBURG, NC 27549
BRANCHES IN BUNN.
FRANKLINTON, & YOUNGSVILLE

Copyright © 1994 by Howard Owen

Library of Congress Cataloging-in-Publication Data

Owen, Howard, 1949–
    Fat lightning / by Howard Owen.
        p.   cm.
    ISBN 1-877946-41-9 : $22.00
    1. Jesus Christ—Apparitions and miracles (Modern)—Fiction.
2. City and town life—Virginia—Fiction. 3. Marriage—Virginia—
Fiction. I. Title.
PS3565.W552F37   1994
813'.54—dc20   93-6339
                                                                CIP

All rights reserved, including the right to reproduce this book,
or parts thereof, in any form, except for the inclusion of brief
quotes in a review.

First Edition: August, 1994 -- 4,000 copies

Manufactured in the United States of America

THE PERMANENT PRESS
Noyac Road
Sag Harbor, NY 11963

YO-ACX-428

FAT LIGHTNING

a novel
by Howard Owen

THE PERMANENT PRESS
Noyac Road
Sag Harbor, NY 11963

FRANKLIN COUNTY LIBRARY
906 NORTH MAIN STREET
LOUISBURG, NC 27549
BRANCHES IN BUNN.
FRANKLINTON, & YOUNGSVILLE